DAY OF THE ARROW

Philip Loraine was the pseudonym of Robin Estridge, a prolific novelist and screenwriter. Born in 1920, Estridge wrote many novels of crime and suspense under the Loraine name and also wrote literary fiction under his own name. He is perhaps best remembered today for *Day of the Arrow* (1964), published under the Loraine pseudonym and adapted by Estridge for the screenplay of the film *Eye of the Devil* (1966), starring David Niven, Deborah Kerr, and Sharon Tate. Robin Estridge died in 2002.

DAY OF THE ARROW

PHILIP LORAINE

VALANCOURT BOOKS

Day of the Arrow by Philip Loraine
First published London: Collins, 1964
First Valancourt Books edition 2015
Reprinted from the 1st U.S. edition (M.S. Mill, 1964)

Published by Valancourt Books, Richmond, Virginia
http://www.valancourtbooks.com

All Valancourt Books publications are printed on acid free paper
that meets all ANSI standards for archival quality paper.

ISBN 978-1-941147-69-6
Also available as an electronic book.

Cover by Lorenzo Princi
Set in Adobe Caslon 10/12.5

I

The Faithless Wife

The woman was coming out of a room at the far end of the corridor. He could never decide, later, whether he had known then and there that it was Françoise; when she turned her head a second later and he saw her face there was not quite the punch of shock that there ought to have been; for this reason he thought that some sixth sense had warned him in the fraction of a moment before her turning.

A man followed her out of the room and shut the door. They smiled at each other, and he took her arm.

James Lindsay stepped back into shadow and shut his eyes. He had always expected that one day, at a corner, wind blowing, or under trees in the evening, he would see Françoise again; there had been no feeling of shock; a sixth sense had lulled him so that he was completely unprepared for the straight left to the jaw—or perhaps, more exactly, the knee jab in the groin: Françoise coming out of a bedroom in the Hotel National et Nord with a lover.

He glanced at them again as they turned out of the corridor towards the elevator. Oh yes, a lover. No doubt about that.

He realized that he was clutching the key of his room so hard that it was hurting his hand. He released it, lifted it up and looked at it. The key, even more than what his eyes had seen, seemed to sum up the situation; summed it up with all the cruel finality of inanimate objects, which will not, like the human mind, adapt themselves to soft answers. It was a large brass key attached by a brass chain to an oval disc on which was the number of the room. The number was engraved very large as if in preparation for the succession of more or less intoxicated eyes which were going to come stumbling in out of the Parisian

5

night in search of it. The key was battered; it had seen life since its Edwardian birth.

Françoise and the man had reached the elevator and were hopefully pressing buttons; but the elevator was of the same period as the key; at that age you do not answer at once and when you do, you are not in a hurry. So that a new line of thought had time to slip into James Lindsay's reeling brain. He was, in fact and humanlike, just searching about for some easy excuse when the battered brass key, at which he was still gazing witlessly, informed him that women like Françoise de Montfaucon, Marquise de Bellac, do not in fact use hotels like the National et Nord for any purpose that is not illicit. The difference, this key informed Lindsay, between himself and Françoise was that, whereas he could not afford to stay in a better hotel, she could not afford to be seen in one; it was at this point that anger took over. He could hear the whining and groaning of the ancient elevator which had at last bestirred itself, but which, like all old hotel servants, was not going to let its trouble go unappreciated. What James Lindsay did next was not gentlemanly and certainly not by any social standard Parisian. He acted, moreover, before there was time to consider. He marched out of his protecting shadow into the corridor, turned right down the passage that led to the elevator, and reached it at exactly the moment when the man was opening the gate for Françoise. She did not therefore see him at all until she had walked into the contraption and had turned. By this time Lindsay and her friend were bowing to each other on a who-precedes-whom basis.

All right, thought Lindsay, I'm a bastard. What of it? He looked up as he stepped into the elevator, and met her eyes.

Her eyes had not changed. He thought again as he had thought so often in the past, Well, if the eyes are really the mirror of the soul, this woman's soul is deep, pure and beautiful; they were dark brown eyes, both exciting and soothing, critical and forgiving. She was clearly horrified to see him at this moment and in these circumstances, yet all that showed of her emotion was a sudden lifelessness. He thought, For her, this is what they call 'a small death.' That was how she looked —as if, suddenly and momentarily, she had died or been turned to stone. She said nothing. Her gentleman friend had by now wrestled the gates shut and was pressing the button which should, if all went well, deliver them to the ground floor.

Knowing that he would now turn to her, and apparently unable to actually remove her eyes from Lindsay's face—much to his gratification—she simply shut them. A second later the man did turn; he said, 'You're tired.' His tone was gentle, his accent unmistakably that of *The* Arrondissement. Lindsay looked at him and could not, with the best will in the world, dislike what he saw: elegant, charming, not too handsome, but with that catlike self-assurance which he envied so much in Frenchmen; it came, he always imagined, from a youth spent in a world where the family was still the pivotal point, the center of the universe, a fortress of love, all protecting— instead of the kind of incompetently run youth hostel it had become in America and England. If Françoise had to take a lover, this man, damn him, was undoubtedly the right one.

She did not open her eyes again until the elevator had shuddered to a problematical standstill more or less on a level with the ground floor. The gates were opened; she walked out; her friend followed. Lindsay suddenly felt as if he were an air-inflated man and somebody had just taken out the cork.

He followed them more slowly towards the door, wondering whether all energy would perhaps desert him before he reached it, causing him to flop, an inert rubber bag roughly the shape of a man, onto the chill marble floor. He managed however to reach the street and, narrowly missing a motor-scooter, the Bar-Tabac on the other side of it.

After a few minutes the cognac took a grip of his stomach and shook some sense into it. He became aware of the altercation, about football, of course, going on at the other end of the zinc counter, of the idiotic bouncing lights of the pinball machine against the wall, of his own face, reflected—appropriately, he thought—among rows of bottles behind the bar.

He said to himself, 'She doesn't like fair men—that's the answer.'

He knew, naturally, that it was not the answer, but he was hurt as well as dismayed by the encounter. What in heaven's name was she doing, anyway? She had succeeded in marrying the man she adored—not only handsome, not only rich, not only titled, but one of the most charming and kindly people in the world. Of course, in his young days he *had* been involved with a long line of beautiful girls. Could it be that he . . . ? The idea of Philippe de Montfaucon's being unfaithful to Françoise was as unreal as the idea of Françoise being unfaithful to him. And yet, there, across the road in the Hotel National et Nord . . . Lindsay shook his head at the bottles.

Her lover was dark, too. He brooded over this for a time, gazing distastefully at the fair reflection among the bottles: fair, square and perhaps rather stupid-looking—handsome in its way, but a bit thick. He nodded at the reflection and ordered another cognac; that was it—a bit of a numbskull. It was a pity, because he was not really a numbskull at all.

James Lindsay at thirty was a promising young painter—or rather a 'promising young painter,' for such a description should never be without its inverted commas. Only two years ago, though no less promising, he had been entirely unknown; his success, for success it was, still surprised him; not that he had been unaware of his own talent, but he had always supposed that it would go unnoticed for at least fifty years. And then two paintings in an exhibition by the Belsize Park Group (he had never lived in Belsize Park, but was said to have affinities with the group; what the affinities were he did not know)—two paintings and one enthusiastic critic, and suddenly there was Mr. F. J. Stein of the Vaga Galleries asking if he had enough stuff for a show of his own. Enough! He had a bed-sitter full of them. It was now that total unreality set in: forty pictures sold out of fifty-one, and a gentleman called Ted Hathaway—one of those perpetually angry old American writers—asking him to illustrate his book, *Europe at Sunset*.

And that was the reason for his being in Paris at all; it was the first capital at which Mr. Hathaway had aimed his guns. After which, Berlin, Rome, Athens, Madrid....

James Lindsay, at thirty, knew that he was a lucky young man. He could hardly believe that only three years ago he had been teaching 'Art' (sic) to the disinterested sons of the new rich at Broadways Preparatory School—and, two weeks later, after a battle royal with the headmaster, washing cups in a coffee shop.

At thirty, also, he could feel that he had vindicated his physical appearance, which, at twenty, had been his despair. At parties in attics, with glasses and girls all over the floor, no one had taken his aspirations seriously—least of all the girls. Youth being the most conservative of institutions, it was impossible for this chunky, pink-faced, fair-haired refugee from a football field to be a creative artist. Creative artists just did not look like that, and everybody knew it. He was not unpopular; indeed many of the girls had thought that in various explicit ways he had more to offer them than the tall, lank, dank and sallow young men whose work they admired. Often he would find himself struggling on divans in darkened rooms when all he wanted to do was discuss Modigliani and Proust until dawn.

And then—for he had studied for two years at the Sorbonne —he had met Françoise....

'Monsieur Leensseye?'

He turned, thinking how improbable his name sounded in French, and found one of the elderly porters of the Hotel National et Nord (same age as the elevator) looking up at him.

'I saw you cross the street,' said this ancient.

Lindsay nodded. He had stayed many times at the hotel; he knew the porters; they had lobster eyes on stalks; they missed nothing.

'Telephone,' said the porter.

Lindsay's stomach contracted. He had arrived in Paris that morning. None of his friends knew that he was there. Only one person had seen him. As if to echo this thought the porter, putting on a weary archness reserved for British and American visitors to Paris, said, 'A lady.'

Lindsay nodded again. For five years he had not seen Françoise, had not heard from her or of her. For five years he had
known at the back of his mind that somewhere they would
meet again, somewhere light would catch that faultlessly
molded cheek, or he would hear the unmistakable laugh in a
crowded room. Well, it had happened; and it had happened
well and truly. There are people with whom you know you are
involved—not just for a day or a year, but forever: until death;
and very possibly beyond it; in fact there is no need even to
see them again because the involvement is in one's own being.
These people mark you and become part of you.

James Lindsay followed the porter back across the street to
the hotel.

'Hullo. James?' She sounded as if she had been running;
also she spoke in a curiously hushed voice as if in a public
place.

He said, 'Yes.'

Silence. He could hear her breathing. He could see, in his
mind's eye, the lovely face framed by the fur collar of that coat.
It was funny that he had not even looked at her clothes, and
yet, now, he could see the faultless coat for which Givenchy or
possibly Balenciaga had fined her something over a thousand
dollars.

At last she said, 'James, I must see you.'

The urgency of this after five years' silence made him laugh.
Françoise was not the sort of woman to whom this laugh had
to be explained.

'No,' she said. 'You must know how it is. I never . . .'

'Thought of me?'

'I have often thought of you, but not ... Foolish of me,
because ... because you are one of the few people I have ever
known who might be able to help me now.'

Suddenly he recognized something very shocking in her
voice. He recognized it because he had once heard it before—
on a foggy night six years ago when she had come hammering
at his door at two in the morning; she had been to a party;
there had been no taxis; crossing the Pont Royal a man had

grabbed her from behind, had tried to rape her. What Lindsay had heard then, what he heard now, was the raw edge of terror.

'What's the matter? Are you in trouble?'

'No. Yes . . . Please, where can I see you? When?'

'Anytime. Anywhere.' And he did not resist the desire to add, 'As always.'

Again there was silence. She was thinking.

'After your dinner,' he suggested, not altogether tactfully but with intention.

'Yes, we are having dinner.'

'I should hope so; he looked civilized.'

Sharply Françoise said, 'Don't be provincial—it doesn't suit you.'

He grimaced to himself, knowing he had deserved this. 'How about the Univers?'

'Very well.' She did not like this personal game—the Univers was where they had last seen each other. Lindsay was a little ashamed of himself, but only a little. 'Very well. The Univers—at eleven. You . . . will be there?'

'Nothing,' said Lindsay, 'could stop me.'

She replaced the receiver. The click said more plainly than words, 'You are being insufferable, but as I need your help it is not for me to say so.'

Yet it was Lindsay himself who regretted his own choice of a meeting place. The Univers, cheap and noisy, pulsating with life and youth, had not changed; but he had changed. He paused on the other side of the street, looking at the big café, at the students spilling in and out of it, shouting to each other, clasping each other, fixing their personalities one upon the other with the devastating frankness of youth, as if they meant to suck each other dry of every thought or emotion that was in them. It was like an ant heap; it contained, for him, the same mysterious but ceaseless motion, alien creatures going about a business that was particularly theirs and nothing whatever to do with him.

He found a small and untenanted table with some difficulty and, as he sat down, thought a little wryly of Françoise entering this house of young bears—the Marquise in her Balenciaga or whatever it was.

But of course he was wrong. France is a civilized country and a beautiful woman is always a beautiful woman. Some of the young girls grimaced to each other over the coat, and some of the young men turned to look at her with appreciation. Françoise herself entered the place in exactly the same way that she would have entered Maxim's or a café in Les Halles—conscious that she was going to be admired.

As she sat down she said, 'It was clever of you to think of this place; everyone is too interested in their own conversations to bother with ours.'

They looked at each other. Lindsay noticed for the first time that there were lines of strain round her eyes—slight, revealing puckering of the muscles. She was more beautiful than she had been five years ago; time had perfected the modeling of brow and cheeks and chin, smoothing away the last blurred planes of young girlhood.

'Well?' she asked. 'How *much* have I changed?'

Lindsay smiled. 'We were sitting about here ...' He looked round. 'Yes, just about here one night; I remember telling you ... Heavens, the things one says at that age! I remember saying that I felt as if I were attached to you by my umbilical cord. You gave me a funny feeling in the guts then, and you still do. How's that?'

'I'd say ...' She examined him. 'I'd say you'd been drinking cognac before dinner, and then had a whole bottle of wine all to yourself.'

He nodded. 'How else do you prepare to meet the only woman you've ever been in love with—really in love—when you know she has a husband, children, I suppose ...'

'Two.'

'A title, a lot of money and an attractive lover.'

'You're not very kind to me.'

'You weren't very kind to *me*.'

Françoise considered this. 'Have you ever considered why I wasn't ... kind—how awful!—to you.'

'Oh, I know why. You were in love with Philippe; I didn't have a chance really. Just as you're in love with whatever his name is, now.'

Françoise let him order coffee for her; she never took her eyes off him. When the waiter had gone away she leaned forward. 'No, James, you are wrong—wrong, I mean, about Daniel.'

'Ah yes, Daniel. Of course. It would be.'

She ignored this. 'I *was* in love with Philippe; perhaps I still am.'

The look that she flashed up at him from under lowered lids made Lindsay bite back the acid retort that this remark seemed to him to deserve. Instead he said, 'Forgive me, but I really have heard that one before.'

She nodded. 'I find your ... scorn difficult to take, James.'

'I'm sorry. I'm jealous.'

Françoise looked away from him. Her voice when she spoke again was flat and colorless. 'I always *could* speak to you. I ... I'm going to tell you something I've never told anyone else. Philippe and I have been married six years. For three years he ... he hasn't touched me; he hasn't come near my bed; he doesn't even sleep in the same room.'

Lindsay had leaned forward, eyes wide.

'Can a woman, a normal, healthy woman who has been awakened sexually ... ? Up to three years ago our relationship was as perfect as could be; I think perhaps we were more like lovers than a husband and wife. Can a woman to whom this has happened be blamed for taking a lover—even one she does not ... love?' She looked up at him and her eyes were bleak; through them he looked into the arctic world of her loneliness, and what he saw caught at his heart.

There was silence while the waiter brought their coffee.

Lindsay said, 'But what does it mean? What's happened to him? Has he got another woman—a mistress?'

'No.' She said it with certainty. 'I was going to say, "I'm

sure," but . . . No, I'm not sure of anything any more. And yet I'd swear there isn't a woman; one can feel that, always.'

'There must be something; you must suspect something.'

'It's Bellac,' she said with surprising passion. 'If he would leave Bellac everything would be all right.'

Lindsay stared at her in amazement. 'Bellac! The family place. He's there?'

'*We*,' she said, 'are there.'

'But he used to laugh about it; he used to say he'd rather die than live there; he used to do wicked imitations of the people and the dialect . . .' He broke off, disturbed by the deep misery of her stare.

'He hasn't left the valley for two years. He isn't living at Bellac, he *is* Bellac. Dear God, how I hate the place.'

Lindsay stared at her in amazement. 'I always thought of you traveling around the world together. I kept seeing your names in the dirt columns, pictures sometimes: "The Marquis and Marquise de Bellac in New York . . . Amalfi . . . Venice . . . Casablanca"—all over the place. Tahiti once, I'm sure.'

Françoise said darkly, 'Yes, we were in Tahiti; we traveled too much, spent too much . . . Oh God, drank too much, lay in the sun too much. I admit that; I even said so to Philippe.'

Lindsay shook his head over this; he could not visualize Philippe as lord of his enormous domain; that faultlessly dressed, witty, always slightly mocking figure would not compose itself into the foreground of an immense pastoral landscape. When people said that the French aristocracy were effete, it was men like Philippe they were thinking of—if, indeed, they were thinking at all. Born to an enormous fortune, his mother the daughter of a Swiss banker, his grandmother a South American heiress, he had liked beautiful women, beautiful pictures, beautiful wine and food, and beautiful places—in that order.

Françoise removed her hand and took a sip of her coffee.

'You were very fond of Philippe, weren't you, James?'

'Yes, I was.'

'Will you help me? Will you help him?'

Lindsay laughed. 'What am I meant to do? Go down to the Auvergne with a spade and dig him out of Bellac?'

Françoise let out a little gasp and almost dropped her coffee cup. Lindsay was appalled to see that her eyes were tight shut, that the color had drained from her face. He thought that she was going to faint, or perhaps had fainted.

The waiter ran forward—however crowded a café, waiters somehow manage to keep an eye on the needs of women like Françoise de Montfaucon. The magnificent coat was wiped, cognac was produced, there was a reassuringly everyday fuss during which something dark receded from the table, and Lindsay realized how strangely the noisy extrovert world around them had dropped away during their conversation, leaving them alone in a place which was not quite real. Indeed, what had he said to bring about this moment of terror? Something about going down to Bellac with a spade and digging . . .

He leaned forward, staring at the woman who sat opposite him. Gradually the fuss around them subsided; the solicitous waiter withdrew. At last Françoise looked up from her small glass of brandy.

Lindsay said, 'Françoise, you don't . . . You can't mean . . . He isn't ill, is he?'

'I don't know what *ill* means.' The flatness of this took his breath away.

'He's in danger?'

The eyes over the brandy glass were composed again, almost withdrawn. 'He . . . he says he is going to die.'

'He says . . . !' Lindsay could not believe his ears.

Françoise said, 'He's as strong as a horse; he admits it, the doctor admits it; in fact, the doctor thinks I'm crazy. But then Philippe hasn't . . . hasn't told *him*.'

'He told *you*?'

'I said to him, "Philippe, I thought I would go and stay with my Aunt Claudine during September." And he . . . he just nodded. So I said, "You won't mind my going?"'

Lindsay could see that she was reliving this conversation

exactly as it had happened; the effort which she was making to be exact was almost pathetic to watch.

'He said to me, "No, why should I mind? I won't be here myself." So you see I was rather excited; I thought, At last he's going away; he's going to leave this dreadful place. I ran to him. I said, "Philippe, I'm so glad. Where are you going?" I said, "It'll do you so much good to get away. Are you sure you wouldn't like me to come too?"'

She was peering into the amber light of her brandy, almost as though she could see the whole scene contained there in miniature.

'Then he turned and looked at me. And it was . . . James, it was such a strange look. He ran his fingers down my cheek; and that was something he hadn't done for years—something he used to do when . . . well, *after* we had made love. He said, "No, I don't want you to come too, little one."'

She stopped speaking and finished her brandy.

Lindsay leaned forward. 'Now wait a minute, Françoise . . .'

She interrupted him passionately. 'It was his voice, it was the *way* he said it. James, you can't love a man and live with him for six years without knowing something of what is in his mind.'

'He never said in so many words that he was going to die.'

She dismissed this with an impatient gesture. 'Look, James, on such and such an evening maybe I ask the Jehan de Marchals to dinner, and I say to Philippe, "Oh darling, by the way, the Marchals are dining tomorrow." And Philippe says, "But, my dear, you know I am going over to see Jacques Lacombe tomorrow about replanting the south shore of the lake." Do you imagine I don't know what he really means? That he can't stand his Cousin Georges, who is always trying to borrow money off him; he knows that I am right to ask them; he simply doesn't intend to be present, that's all.' She gazed at him almost fiercely, and Lindsay, against all rational thought, knew that she might very well be right. Everything she said gave him a fresh glimpse into a world of which he knew nothing—a glimpse of a Philippe de Montfaucon of whom he knew nothing.

Françoise laid both her hands palms downward on the marble top of the table and looked at them severely; it was as if, by this study of two objects so well known to her, she could in some way calm herself. 'Very well,' she said. 'I will tell you the end of it. During this conversation—about his going away—he was sitting at his desk. Naturally when he had said this appalling thing ... No, James, there was no mistaking it. He said, "No, I don't want you to come too, little one." And his voice was ... oh, empty, desolate, as if already he were speaking to me from a long way off. And then the touch of his fingers ...' She raised one of her own slim hands to her cheek, reliving that touch.

'James, I was horrified; I know what people mean when they say their blood ran cold. I took hold of him, and I think I almost shouted at him—it's difficult for you to realize how, at Bellac ... My nerves used to be so strong. I said to him, "Philippe, what do you mean?" And he didn't answer. I think I probably shook him, and I asked again, "What do you mean?" Then he stood up, James, and he took my wrists—he's terribly strong, did you know that?—and he sort of bent me away from him. His face was hard, a stone face.' Her fingers felt the wrist of the other hand. 'He hurt me. He walked straight out of the room. And it was then, you see, that I looked down at his desk.' She broke off, and said, 'James, I'd like some more cognac.'

Lindsay summoned the waiter and ordered the brandy. Françoise shook her head as if to clear away the evil things that clouded her brain. 'You know the crest, you must have seen it in the old days: on that fob, on his signet ring?'

Lindsay nodded. 'The falcon. Montfaucon.'

'Yes. Well, naturally it's at the head of our notepaper. There was a pile of notepaper on his desk, and he had drawn something while he was talking to me—without thinking or even intentionally, I don't know.' She looked up, her eyes very dark, very pained. 'He had drawn an arrow through the falcon, James.'

2

The White Bird

James Lindsay was not a man for prospects; being Scottish by extraction he had been spoon-fed too many mountains, lakes and torrents in infancy; when there is no basis of comparison, size hardly matters—and, anyway, to a child everything seems too large. So there it was—Loch Tay or Lago di Como, Ben Nevis or the Matterhorn, he preferred a crooked street or a well-worn face, or a glimpse of a hot sea through a shuttered window.

However, it has to be a very hardened traveler who can take the road from Ussel to Aurillac and not find himself pausing now and again to stare at the gothic peaks of the Auvergnes or at the shimmering Dordogne far below among crags and perilously leaning pines, the river of all fairy tales.

Lindsay stopped the small Renault which he had hired, and walked out onto a dizzy bluff poised between mist-wreathed mountains and dull, pewter river; it was an overcast, warm, ominous day. He sat down and regarded the prospect, but after a few minutes he no longer saw it, for his mind was turned inwards. He had been impelled to stop as much by the desire to do some soul-searching as by the gloomy magnificence of the view.

His motives for taking this journey were suspect, that was the trouble; and he was too honest a person simply to shut the lid on suspect motives and sit on them. Honesty apart, he knew from past experience that if you did this the motives had a way of working on themselves like rotten refuse, or like wine bottled too young. An explosion followed. Therefore he sat, frowning at the River Dordogne but not seeing it.

Very well then—Françoise. The fascination she held for him had not abated one iota, rather the reverse; moreover, he could not help feeling that in what she had told him there were evasions and omissions, some intentional; this, of course, increased the fascination. So—he must be honest: he had agreed to make this journey to Bellac because he wanted to see more of her. And then, Philippe. He had to admit that a driving, gnawing curiosity impelled him towards this man, some facet of whom he had once called friend. Yes, indeed, friend. In those golden days of their early youth the two of them had been inseparable; they had not only shared an apartment, they had shared life, carving off chunks of it and eating as much as they could stomach. Françoise had said, repeatedly, how well she knew her husband; undoubtedly, because he was her husband, what she said was true. Yet there are things in a man that only another man can recognize, and that a woman—no matter whether she be wife or mother—is blind to.

Curiosity, then, and a desire to be near Françoise impelled him towards Bellac. What else? Continuing in honesty, he doubted—even if the fantastic situation she imagined really did exist—whether he could help her. Gazing into her eyes in that café, full of students, islanded with her amongst that alien din, he had been strangely convinced. Next morning, already committed to making this fantastic journey, he could not help feeling that maybe she was the one whose brain needed a rest and possibly treatment. How embarrassing, he thought, if on arrival at the Chateau de Bellac he found this to be the case: some grizzled and kindly family doctor leading him aside—into the library; it was always the library—and explaining that poor dear Françoise . . . since she had lost that child. . . .

Lindsay shook his head at the Dordogne, frowning.

But she had a lover—of that there was no doubt—and he had not been able to resist asking her why, if she needed help so badly, she had not turned to the elegant and self-assured Daniel. Her reply, though what the Anglo-Saxons would call 'very French,' was unarguably right. *Because* Daniel had been her lover, he could never be asked for help; he was a friend of Philippe's; he would not, of course, have been able to refuse her, but think of his position! At Bellac! In Philippe's own house! Françoise had only been a little irritated by Lindsay's laughter. Besides—and this had probably been the best part of the whole conversation for him—she did not trust Daniel; she knew the world he lived in; she knew how delicious a morsel it would be: 'You haven't heard? My dear, Philippe de Montfaucon has to be *kept* down at Bellac. No, dear, not exactly dangerous. But you remember his Uncle Antoine. One feels sorry for *her*, poor thing.'

Lindsay looked up at the mountains, immense in the mist that wreathed them; he grimaced at them. He stood up and stretched—he was a little too large for the small Renault—and he spoke aloud to the peaks and the pines and the pewter river far below. 'I'm curious,' he said. 'By God, I am curious. Also I love Françoise, I always have. Come to that, I suppose I love Philippe too. Or did.'

He shook his head over Love, which in youth can embrace so much so gallantly and which the passing of time, and the grubbiness of humanity, can tarnish so quickly. Then he went back to the car.

After the little town of Dennat, where he had an excellent meal, finding the way became complicated. The three people whom he asked all had very clear notions of the best route but all their ideas were different; there was a quick way, a beautiful way, an easy way; between the three Lindsay lost himself four times. When he finally came to the sturdy, discreet wooden arrow pointing up a side road and emblazoned with the one word *Bellac*, it was only to realize that he had in fact passed it not half an hour before, going in the opposite direction.

The first five miles were easy; the road surface was good, the sun emerged from behind lowering clouds, birds sang, and the plateau of bracken and heather growing amongst forests of giant boulders seemed a friendly place. Then suddenly, with no warning, there was a sharp right turn and the road appeared to vanish altogether. Appalled, Lindsay jammed on the brakes; he raised himself in the seat and looked over the edge. He discovered that the road did not in fact come to an abrupt end, though it did the next best thing; it plunged into a ravine with a series of hair-raising corkscrew twists. Lindsay slipped into bottom gear and advanced.

Immediately the landscape changed; vegetation vanished except for a few brave weeds which had somehow found soil among the crannies of the smooth, sheer cliffs.

Water had done this, Lindsay realized. The boulder-strewn plateau had in reality been the bed of a vast river at some lost point in time; and the river, coming to this cliff, had at first thundered over in a prehistoric Niagara; later, wearing and wearing the rock, it had tunneled for itself this hellish gorge. When at last the road straightened out sufficiently to allow him to look upwards Lindsay was horrified, because he was to a slight degree subject to claustrophobia, to see that the sky had gone away from him and was now a bright slit framed by towering cliffs of limestone. The road shared the bottom of this ravine with what had once been the river and was now—in July, at least—a cowed-looking stream.

He was glad when, after another two miles, the gorge began to open out; trees reappeared—pines and oaks and mountain ash. Still, however, the road ran downhill, twisting and turning along the line of the ancient riverbed. Then, suddenly, it shot off at a tangent, plunged into the gloomiest forest of fir trees that even Lindsay, a Scot, had ever seen, and finally flung him out into a burst of sunshine and his first tremendous sight of Bellac. He stopped the car and got out.

Where the ancient river had curved round a great pine-clad bluff there now lay a beautiful sickle-shaped lake; on the opposite shore to the bluff was a smiling valley, a bowl of sunny fields and coppices some seven or eight miles across; above the fields vineyards climbed the lower slopes of the hills, and above the vineyards were more trees and rocky outcrops, and above the rocks—but in some way removed and no longer menacing —were the peaks of the Cevennes or the Auvergnes, he was not sure which. And at the far end of the lake, cushioned in this green bowl, was the Chateau de Bellac, turrets and towers shining in a patch of sunlight, golden-gray stone against shadowed trees beyond.

Aloud, Lindsay said, 'Well!'

After this moment of excitement, of elation, doubt came tumbling into his mind; he would dearly have liked to turn round and drive back to Paris. Suddenly, faced with this castle gleaming like an ancient jewel in a bed of green velvet, he *knew* that he had dreamed his meeting with Françoise and everything that she had told him. He turned and looked with distaste at the little car, at the litter of his painting things in the back seat; he thought, his stomach dropping away from him, of the telegram—that absurd telegram worked out so carefully with Françoise at a table in the Café de l'Univers in the Boulevard Saint Michel in Paris, France: 'Saw in papers you were in residence stop will you remember me if I appear Tuesday afternoon stop James Lindsay.'

Now, looking down at Bellac, he trembled to think of it; it would not deceive a child of six. Françoise had said, 'Don't fuss, James. Telegrams are always brought to me. No one will even *see* it but me.'

Lindsay grimaced to himself. Madame la Marquise was very sure of herself. Faced with the smiling pleasance before him he could only hope that Madame la Marquise was not off her beautiful nut.

In this mood James Lindsay got into his hired Renault and drove down into the valley towards the chateau. He had not gone more than a few hundred yards before the first of his surprises took place. There was a screech in his left ear like three trumpets played fortissimo out of key, he wrenched the Renault onto the grass verge, and a long, low, white Mercedes howled past him and vanished round the corner ahead. Apart from being glad that he had not had to try conclusions with this vehicle on any hairpin bends, Lindsay could not equate the car with his preconceptions about Bellac; the driver had been very fair, so it had not been Philippe; Françoise had, perhaps unwittingly, given him the impression of a rural-monastic life, miles from civilization. How exactly did the white Mercedes fit into this picture? It would be interesting to find out.

The road now wound its way down into the valley, passing among the vineyards, where the usual bent figures, so brown and so bent that they might have been carved out of the vines which they were tending, raised their heads to stare at his passing. The air was heavy, heady with what he could only suppose was the scent of ripe grapes. And yet, in July ... ? He was puzzled, and very slightly sickened: it was not a pleasant smell. In a few minutes, however, the vineyards were replaced by meadows, running along the side of the lake; lazy cows stood up to their stomachs in long grass, chewing and chewing, and flicking the flies off each other with their tails. It was all pastoral, all peace.

He came at length to the village of Bellac—quite a large village, he was surprised to see—cowering at the foot of the mound on which stood the castle. There was a small square on the main street: plane trees, and an ancient church, even a café with some rickety-looking tables outside it. Nothing outstanding, nor even especially beautiful, but there was certainly not the atmosphere of murky gloom for which his conversation with Françoise had prepared him. And yet ... Yet what?

He drew the Renault to a standstill in the square and sat frowning, listening. Listening to what? Exactly! A silence such as he could not remember before. Nonsense; it was the inevitable silence that succeeded the noise of the car, mile after mile of car noise. In a few seconds his ears would grow accustomed to it, and the small sounds of everyday life would slowly return; there would be the clucking of hens somewhere, and a mooing from the fat cows along the lakeside, for it could not be far off milking time; there would be ...

But he listened—and there was nothing.

Perhaps, he thought, this is some strange atmospheric condition peculiar to the place: the silence of Bellac. It sounded good. He got out of the car and walked across the square. His footsteps resounded, clanged back at him from the stone walls of the houses. A lace curtain stirred; someone was looking at him. The sun was hot suddenly; it lay in thick glowing slabs across the cobbles of the square; he felt that if he walked on the sunlight it would give softly underfoot.

Well, he thought, all agricultural towns are quiet by day when the men, and probably half the women and children too, are out in the fields working.

But even as he got back into the car he knew that this was an excuse made to cover up uneasiness. It was almost with a sense of relief that he drove out of the village towards the chateau. The view of it that he had seen first, from the other end of the lake, had shown him a late seventeenth- or early eighteenth-century façade—a façade not unprepared for trouble, but on the other hand not stern enough to make a bad background for pleasure. The side that he now approached had been built for war and only for war. Two massive towers flanked a drawbridge, and, beyond, great bastions of masonry soared up to a frowning brow of battlements. Only then was a little frivolity allowed to break out in the form of ornamented pepper pots glued to the battlements, and a cluster of slender towers capped with pointed hats of slate, each vying with the other in the absurdity of the weathervanes surmounting them.

Lindsay thought that the total effect would have been grim indeed were it not for the saving grace of the stone which had built it; the stone seemed, even in shadow, to contain a golden light of its own.

The little car rattled impudently over the drawbridge, under a cavernous gateway, beneath the jaws of a portcullis, and into the Cour d'Honneur.

This courtyard was wholly delightful because here the austerity was broken by trees—a square of pollarded plane trees forming a cool green walk all round the perimeter. White doves cooed and fluttered among the leaves or swooped against the golden walls. To one side of the great bulk of the chateau was a huge archway through which could be seen a formal garden, a green lawn sweeping down towards the lake.

Lindsay, getting out of the car, wondered for a moment what might have become of the white Mercedes, which he had expected to find parked in front of the castle. He was also just beginning to experience that sensation in the pit of the stomach which always preluded arrivals at new places. What happened next put an abrupt end to all that. There was a sad, protesting squawk from above his head and he was aware of something falling on him. Instinctively he stepped back. A fluttering bundle of white feathers dropped at his feet—a white dove threshing around in its death agonies. A moment later, and it lay still.

Lindsay stared at the dead bird with more than ordinary interest, for he was remembering something that Françoise had said.

A sudden laugh made him glance up. A young man stood in the great archway that gave into the formal garden. In his hand he held a full-sized bow; a quiver of arrows was slung over one shoulder. As far as Lindsay could see against the glow of the sunlit garden beyond, he had black hair, the hair of a Florentine page of the Renaissance, close-cut and curling; he seemed to be smiling. He turned and was gone.

Lindsay looked down at the dead dove, eyes now glazing over—the dead dove with the arrow piercing its white body.

3

The Secret Tower

Françoise led him towards a mulberry tree which cast a pool of green shade at the edge of the lawn. The afternoon had become very hot—the solid heat which occurs in sheltered valleys and which usually precedes thunder. The lawn seemed to Lindsay to have grown larger since they started on their way across it; he was suddenly almost too weary to go a step further; but this, of course, was as much to do with his hatred of meeting new people as with the heat.

The two women who sat in the shade of the mulberry tree, an immaculately white tea table laid before them, watched their approach without speaking. Lindsay could feel their eyes pressed up against his face like the suckers of some clammy sea creature.

Françoise saluted them with a casual wave as they drew nearer; both, as if the same thread controlled their two hands, made marionette's gestures by way of reply. They never took their eyes off Lindsay's face, however. By the time he reached the table he was sweating.

Françoise said, 'Betty, this is James Lindsay. James—the Comtesse de Vignon. Tante Estelle, this is James—you've heard Philippe speak of him.'

Aunt Estelle said, 'Indeed yes.' But her eyes were blank, and Lindsay suspected Françoise of indoctrination.

The Comtesse de Vignon said, 'The painter fellow.' She said it in the petrified accents of the English shires.

'Betty,' Françoise explained, very unnecessarily, 'is English too.'

Irritated by her, Lindsay said, 'I'm Scottish.'

The Comtesse Betty examined him minutely from the top of his fair head, via the average presentability of his face, the evidently satisfactory width of his shoulders, general height, stance, to the muscular calf showing against the stuff of his trousers; it was the look she would have given a horse. At the end of it she said, 'Why don't you sit down?'

Lindsay sat down—as far away from her as possible.

Tante Estelle embarked upon what appeared to be a pre-prepared dissertation on Manet, who was clearly her favorite painter. Her voice, like her appearance, was pale gray, a kind of thistledown silver gray that seemed to be in danger of floating away on the next breath of wind. Her age might have been anything between forty and seventy; her fairish, silverish hair was rather attractively dressed on top of her head, with soft wings framing her pale face—an exquisite, attenuated, wistful face; vague, silvery eyes, a long, thin nose, a girl's mouth, a little wishbone of a chin. Lindsay could hardly keep his painter's eyes off her; she was wearing a kind of gray mauve; she reminded him of a fabulous moth, and her conversation was schizophrenic. Whatever she may have been thinking about, it was certainly not Manet. Occasionally, which made Lindsay like her all the more, she darted tiny envenomed looks at Betty, Comtesse de Vignon.

Lindsay decided that Tante Estelle might have determined to look and behave like an aristocratic spinster aunt of no importance, but that in fact she was something quite different. (He had not yet had time to understand that everyone at Bellac was something different from what he seemed.)

Countess Betty, in the meantime, was saying to Françoise, 'Anyway, I am *not* going to Venice, and I told them so. I said if they *had* to go to Dubrovnik I'd join them there in September. I said, "It'll be *swarming* with Poly Tours and all the rest of it, and personally I don't think you'll stay there a week." Of course, when they're at home they live in Chelsea, so they're used to that sort of thing; I find her common. Do you?'

Françoise said, 'I find her dull.'

Lindsay became aware of something: they were, all four of them, people in a waiting room—people in a foyer—people passing the time in anticipation of something which is about to happen. The knowledge, curiously, gave him a slight prickling feeling down the spine, and he glanced over his shoulder.

Tante Estelle was saying, '... But then take Boudin; movement can be contained in the tiniest space. Look at my ring.' She suddenly thrust under his nose a magnificent ruby solitaire. The sun caught it; captured suns, blood-red at nightfall, dazzled him, whirling in space. She snatched the ring away and said, in the same tone of voice, 'They will come.'

Lindsay stared at her, amazed, but she was shooting another mildly murderous look at the Comtesse.

That lady, stretching out long, riding legs, encased in tight white trousers, said, 'Darling, I'm dying for tea. Are we waiting for someone?'

At this, most disconcertingly, Tante Estelle caught Lindsay's eye and gave him a faint smile of complicity. Although she fascinated him, he began to wish he was sitting somewhere else. He became aware of Françoise gazing absently at him; she was saying, 'I don't think we shall be seeing Philippe until dinner.'

She was answered by a voice out of the yew hedge behind her. 'Not even at dinner; he asked me to tell you.'

Tante Estelle snorted.

A moment later the young man with the bow and arrow came into view round the corner of the hedge. He was indeed, as Lindsay had thought, very dark, Italianate; but now, no longer framed in shadow by the archway—no longer gaining stature from the unexpected and distinctly sinister incident of the shot dove—he seemed merely a handsome boy in a red shirt and crumpled fawn trousers, a little sulky perhaps.

The Comtesse Betty gave him her analytical look and said, 'Christian, you look a mess.'

The boy gave her a look of equal directness and replied, 'Maman, I *am* a mess.' But he bent, rather surprisingly, and kissed Françoise on the cheek. 'You smell marvelous,' he said. 'What is it?'

Lindsay was not by any means an ingenuous person, but the information that this young man was the son of the Countess Betty really did take his breath away; he looked with a little more interest at the slim, almost stringy woman in the white trousers with her blank oval of a face on which the features seemed to have been stuck after casual selection from a box labeled *Average:* one nose, feminine; two eyes, ordinary brown with eyebrows attached; one mouth, non-committal.

Her son threw his bow onto the grass, slipped the quiver off his shoulder and came to the chair next to Lindsay; he sat down, turned, and gave a prolonged and interested stare. There was nothing Lindsay could do but return it. He found himself looking into two eyes which were unmistakably but quite subtly of different colors; the left one was a greenish blue, the right one, basically the same color, was flecked with amber; the effect was attractive but disconcerting, and it was clear that Master Christian liked it that way—for having made his mark, he gave a very small smile and looked away.

Tante Estelle said, 'Now, Lindsay, as a painter, do you find that Christian has an interesting face?'

And while Lindsay was seeking the right words, she added,

'Christian finds that Christian has an interesting face, but don't be influenced by that.'

Françoise said, 'Betty, your wish is granted. Tea.'

However, neither her intervention nor the rather absurd procession of menials approaching across the lawn was going to stop Tante Estelle and young Christian from finishing their verbal scuffle.

'Mlle. de Montfaucon,' said the boy, 'does not like young people.'

He had leaned right across Lindsay to say this, and Lindsay, using his painter's eye, took in the line of the young neck, the cruel smile of youth, the delicacy of the ear and the brightness of the almost black hair. This perfection, for he was certainly an unusually handsome creature, and this concentration of venom upon a woman so much older than himself, were more than disconcerting—they were almost tragic.

Tante Estelle replied, 'Oh, but you are wrong. I am very fond of *young* people.'

The Comtesse Betty gave a neigh of laughter. 'Estelle, you *are* absurd—Christian's only eighteen.' Her son flashed her a look of unadulterated scorn. Tea arrived.

'For God's sake,' said Lindsay, striding restlessly round his bedroom, 'who are they? What are they doing here?'

Françoise was sitting in an ancient and beautifully carved chair by the window. 'They've upset you.' She said it with satisfaction.

Lindsay turned, leaning against the foot of the fourposter. 'Françoise, you're behaving like a clam; don't imagine for a moment I don't know why.'

All he got for this was a nod.

'You want me to get the atmosphere of the place, don't you? Well, please believe me, I have.'

'Betty,' said Françoise quietly, 'is one of the ... the friends we made during our traveling years. At first she seems to be an idiot, but she is not; she has that strange English quality of loyalty. She married Pierre when she was very young; she

hardly ever sees him—he spends most of his time in the Afri-
can jungle, as you probably know ...'

'Oh, *that* de Vignon—the one who lives among the lepers.'

'Yes. It's ... not easy to bring up a boy without a father.'

Lindsay said, 'That boy, anyway. But what are they doing
here?'

'Philippe asked them. She wants to buy one of his horses.'

'And where is Philippe?'

Maddeningly, she shrugged. 'How should I know?' Then,
seeing the look of irritation on Lindsay's face: 'Tante Estelle
is his father's sister—you probably guessed that; they were
devoted to each other. When he was drowned she came to live
here permanently; she has a suite of her own, her own maid.
She's no trouble, but she's got a few odd little ways like all old
people.'

'So I noticed.'

A faint, almost wistful smile greeted this. 'No, she doesn't
like Christian.'

'I wonder why.'

'Try asking her; it might be interesting.'

Impatiently, Lindsay went over to the window and took her
by the shoulders. 'Françoise. My dear. I agree with you that
there's an ... atmosphere here; the place is strange, unsettling;
you seem to have surrounded yourself with weird people. I can
imagine that if I lived here for a long time I'd ... I'd imagine
things myself.'

'Imagine! Ah.' Her eyes were suddenly alight, burning; he
realized that he had been led by her silence to say the thing
she had been waiting for him to say. She stood up abruptly,
wrenching his hands from her shoulders; and now it was she
who began to prowl restlessly about the room. 'I suppose I
imagine the fact that my husband ...' She turned on him, her
voice rising. 'James, I loved Philippe; I loved him in every way;
I needed him; my heart needed him and my body needed him.
You can't understand what it was like—in the beginning I
thought I would go mad. When you love someone that person
becomes part of you ...'

'I know that.'

'And when that person withdraws himself—oh, but absolutely, James. Do you understand what I mean by that? You can touch the person, speak to him, kiss him if you feel like it, but the person, the interior of the person, has gone.' She threw back her head and gave a terrifying gasp of laughter. 'Am I the kind of woman who wants to take lovers?'

'No.'

'Then how dare you ... how dare you suggest that I imagine ...' She broke off, her voice faltering; she put her beautiful hands over her face and turned away from him.

Desperately Lindsay wanted to go to her, to take her in his arms; he did not dare—it was as simple as that. He did not dare.

But he was right; his instincts usually were. After a moment she turned back to him and held out a hand. 'Handkerchief, please.'

He gave her one. She blew her nose. 'I'm sorry. Thank you for not ... not touching me. How well we understand each other! We always did.'

Lindsay turned to the window and looked out at the shadows lengthening across the lawn below. He said, 'All the time you spoke of Philippe you used the past tense.'

Behind him there was silence. After a time he turned and looked at her. She had regained her self-possession, and the eyes that met his were non-committal.

'Did I?' she said. 'I must go and change for dinner.'

'No. Wait—please.' He went over to where she stood by the door and looked at her closely. 'What do you, in your deepest heart, think has happened ... is happening to Philippe?'

She shook her head numbly, and the gesture was more explicit than words. It told him of every conceivable explanation, and many that were not conceivable, examined and discarded, and re-examined and again discarded during the endless hours of sleepless nights.

'Françoise, you must tell me what you have thought; I don't know how I can help you, anyway, but without a clue ...'

She nodded, but still said nothing.

'Perhaps he *is* ill; perhaps he has been told ... Forgive me, but, say ... cancer.'

'The doctor examined him. He was out riding—riding round and round his damned estates; sometimes he's away two nights; you've no idea how much he owns, it's a small kingdom.' She moved away from the door, went to the bed and rested her forehead against one of the carved posts. 'Anyway, he fell. He wasn't badly hurt, but of course he had to see the doctor, and I made it an excuse ... Dr. Chauvet is an old friend; he frightened Philippe into having X-rays, blood tests. No, there's nothing wrong with him in that way.' She looked round the room as if seeing it for the first time. 'Perhaps I was wrong to ask you here, my dear James.' Suddenly she looked directly at him with a surprising, disconcerting tenderness. 'Perhaps I was wrong—you're an innocent.' She shook her head. 'Ah yes, and I'm forgetting: that's *why* I asked you here. Don't make me tell you what goes on in my poor aching head; look for yourself, decide for yourself, and then ... Then, if you tell me again that I'm imagining things—that it is I who am crazy ...' She smiled very sweetly at him. '... I won't be angry.'

She held out a hand, and he took it, touched by the softness of it, the defenseless feel of a small hand.

Françoise said, 'Oh, why ... ?' She never said it, but he knew that she had been going to speak of their youth and of the countless, countless times he had asked her to marry him—yes, even in front of Philippe, who had smiled his knowing smile. Instead she said, 'I really must go and see the children; they've been kept out of the way all day, and they do so hate it.'

'When do *I* see them?'

'Now if you like. Come along as soon as you're ready.'

Lindsay laughed. 'No. You wait while I put on a tie; I can't even find my way to the staircase, let alone the nursery.'

Françoise watched him with the affectionate exasperation which seizes women when they are forced to witness the vagaries of the male toilet; she would not have thought twice about keeping him waiting an hour while she changed her entire dress and make-up that went with it, but because he had to make three attempts to shape his bow tie to his satisfaction her foot was quite soon tapping the polished floor.

Together they went along the corridor, stone-flagged, echoing, down a flight of stairs, across a wide landing where six angry-looking Montfaucons gazed down upon them from the walls, up another flight of stairs, through a heavy oak door, and into another wing of the castle.

Glancing out of one of the windows that lit the long passage in which they now found themselves, Lindsay caught a glimpse of a courtyard which he had not seen before, and in it the flash of something white and shining; it was the Mercedes. He turned, the question on his lips, to Françoise, who was at that moment opening the door to the nursery quarters. The sight of her face killed the question stone dead; he could have sworn that in that instant she was mortally afraid of something, yet even as he caught this expression, it changed—Françoise changed it by an effort of the will. She turned to him with a small half-smile and said, 'Philippe's here.'

The Marquis de Bellac was sitting on the floor of the big, friendly room, telling a fairy story; a small boy was clinging round his neck, looking over his shoulder, and a smaller, rather fat little girl was kneeling in front of him, gazing up into his face in open-mouthed wonder. Becoming aware of the intruders—because there was no doubt that this was what they were—all three of them turned, staring.

Philippe smiled. 'James! You haven't changed at all.' He stood up, scattering his children. The little girl ran to her mother, shouting, 'It *was* the Black Cat who hid the ring; I told you it was.'

Shaking hands, Philippe said, 'You should have come to see us before. Are you still painting? Shall I commission you to do a portrait of these two? No, they'd never sit still.'

He had not, Lindsay noticed, lost the habit of starting and finishing a conversation by himself, as if despairing of anyone else ever getting it done quickly enough.

'Yes, I paint—on and off,' he said, pleased to feel such

warmth in this man who had once been his friend, pleased to feel a reciprocated warmth in himself. For a moment, glancing at Françoise, who was whispering to the little girl, he even felt the old, deep-seated antagonism—the antagonism of men for women, who must always complicate their simple friendships with desires, fears, questions.

The small girl, acting presumably on the whispered instructions, came forward and executed a somewhat unsteady curtsey. With a flourish her father introduced her. 'This is Antoinette. Five years old—gargantuan appetite, which accounts for her unfashionable shape—insatiable love of flattery and tall stories.'

They shook hands ceremoniously. The small boy, scowling, marched forward, bowed stiffly and offered his hand.

'Gilles,' said his father. 'Aged six—distinguished astral explorer—expert horseman and show jumper.'

The boy flashed him a delighted grin at this latter allusion. Françoise explained, 'He did all six fences this afternoon without falling off.'

Antoinette said, 'I ride too.' She added proudly, for Lindsay's benefit, '*I* fell off.'

'You bounced,' her father said. 'You're so fat, you bounced.'

The child squealed with delight.

Lindsay found himself in the grip of unreality. Mother, father, two delightful children—all handsome, rich, smiling; and yet she had spoken of death, of secret fears, of her husband's not having touched her for three years. He glanced at her face, and was appalled by the almost ferocious look of guarded calm on it. He looked at Philippe, and was aware of the fact that he had not, indeed, directed a look or a word to his wife. He was saying, 'James, it's good to see you—you look as if you'd just walked out of Eleven Rue Jaquinot.' (This was the address of the apartment they had shared together.) He put an arm round Lindsay's shoulder and turned to his wife. 'He hasn't changed, has he?'

'Not a bit.'

Yes, Lindsay thought, it was true what she had said. The

words they spoke to each other had the flat resonance of a pretense; nothing lay behind them.

Françoise, as if this were unbearable for her, gathered up the children. 'Come,' she said. 'Time to get ready for bed.' A young nursemaid came forward from the far side of the room.

Gilles said, 'It's always bedtime when new people come.'

Antoinette, essaying another curtsey, said, 'Will you paint my picture?'

Her father gathered her up and smacked her plump behind. 'Minx,' he said. There were squeals of delight.

Lindsay was watching the nursemaid, transfixed by the look which she had turned on her master—a look of blind adoration which it was almost embarrassing to witness. Inwardly he grimaced to himself, thinking, Oh well, I suppose it's a tradition to adore the noble Marquis. And yet he was uncomfortably aware that this cliché did not quite fit the case—or the look. A tangent thought, perhaps a memory, tried to express itself in his brain, but he could not quite grasp it. He wondered suddenly about the servants in the chateau. If all that Françoise had said were true—if, indeed, her husband had moved into a separate room three years ago—there must have been some wild surmise below stairs, he a handsome thirty, and she a ravishing twenty-five.

The vague curiosity he had felt was beginning to sharpen itself. He found that he believed almost everything Françoise had said, though he was aware of much that she had left unsaid; also he was beginning to feel the exasperation, almost the fury which people like this produced in him: people who had a perfect life at their fingertips, but who seemed incapable of taking advantage of it. The application with which human beings always seemed to set about destroying their happiness really was immoral. Suddenly he thought, Damn them, they must be mad. I'll get to the bottom of this little mess if it kills me.

Philippe de Montfaucon was saying good night to his children. Lindsay might not have changed in his eyes, but he himself had certainly changed. He had grown thinner, but this had improved his features; he was now remarkably handsome; he reminded Lindsay of some portrait: yes, a Velásquez portrait of a young nobleman or even, possibly, of a young and noble priest. He turned now, smiling, and said, 'James, we'll go riding tomorrow. I'll show you Bellac; we can talk. Do you like riding? Yes, of course you do; I remember.'

Françoise turned, halfway across the room with the children. 'Philippe, you're coming down to dinner?'

'My dear, I can't. I have work to do. Boutet is bringing up his accounts.'

The face he turned to his wife was courteous, but cold—without passion; yet as it came round to Lindsay again warmth returned to it. What was it she had said? 'The *interior* of the person is gone.' Yes, that was it exactly.

Yet so devious are human relationships—so prone to little flatteries, jealousies, blindnesses—that at this moment Lindsay was appalled to find himself thinking, What has she done to make him like this? Immediately he was ashamed; he knew at once that this was only something inside himself responding to Philippe's strong personality, the charm that went with it.

'I'd love to be taken on a conducted tour of your kingdom,' he said.

For an instant something shadowed the handsome face, and was banished. He said, 'We'll have a gossip. Are any of them left in Paris—Didier, or Jean-Françoise, that awful woman Olga ...' He laughed. 'Oh, it's good to see you, James.' He glanced at his watch. 'I must go. There'll be drinks down on the terrace. Have you met Betty yet? Isn't she terrifying? Yet put her on a horse and she becomes a goddess. Well, don't believe it, but I assure you it's true. Give my regards to Christian; tell him to behave himself. Do you know the way? Back through the oak door, straight down that staircase and turn sharp left. See you tomorrow.'

Left alone, Lindsay looked back for Françoise; but she had gone off with her children. Philippe had disappeared through a heavy door at the far end of the passage. Again Lindsay was aware of how quiet it was. He could not decide whether his nerves were responsible for this, or whether, in fact, there was in this whole place a kind of intensity of silence which he had not encountered anywhere else. He was curious suddenly to know where his host had gone—what sort of retreat he had created for himself in this enormous stronghold of his ancestors.

The door, iron-studded, at the end of the passage told him nothing; he moved to one of the windows and looked out. He could see now that the door must lead into what had once been the ancient keep of the castle—possibly in its earliest days—for the tower, although high and massive, had not been conceived on the same vast scale as the rest of the building. Only at the top of it were there any real windows. Yes, it was very old; it had the heavy, rocklike quality of primitive architecture, hewn rather than built.

Lindsay opened the window and leaned out. The small courtyard below him was also very old; here, he was sure, was the original center of the chateau, almost unused now (there was a line of newly washed tablecloths hanging across one corner), brooding over its ancient secrets. The sparkling white Mercedes looked impudent standing in the middle of it.

Lindsay was aware of a chill in the warm evening. He remembered how, two summers ago, he had climbed the hill at Mycenae, had come upon that ancient palace of doom; he realized that this courtyard and keep affected him in the same way—death was here, a long memory of blood.

And Philippe de Montfaucon, Marquis de Bellac, had told his wife ... No! Lindsay banged a fist onto the window ledge, hurting it. He had *not* told his wife that he was going to die. Some alchemy of stress and intuition and the shades of inflection in a known voice had told her so. There was no kind of evidence. No evidence whatsoever. And yet Lindsay, leaning at this window, feeling the weight of the past that thrust up at him from these ancient stones, could indeed believe that what she had felt was right. Death was a germ in the brain of every living man; and here at Bellac, and particularly in this one part of Bellac, death seemed very close, very . . . Ah! Yes that was it. Very *personal*, almost friendly.

He was jerked out of these reflections by a movement below him. A door at the base of the massive tower was opening. Instinctively—how quickly a secret place infects one with its secrecy—Lindsay withdrew his head from the window. Yes, this door led directly onto a spiral staircase; he could just see the bottom two steps. He had, of course, expected Philippe to appear; but it was girl, a slim, almost boyish girl of perhaps eighteen. She wore a sweater and tight black trousers; he thought that she might well have been the sister of the boy Christian, except that whereas his hair was black, hers was very fair, almost white. It was a moment before he recognized her, with a sense of shock, as the driver of the Mercedes. Yet he could forgive himself for having thought that the car was driven by a man; he remembered that she had been wearing some kind of hat, probably a beret, and in any case the remarkable hair was cut short like a boy's so that the head, which was beautifully poised, seemed to be wearing a helmet of bright gold.

She was moving now towards her car; at the same moment, Lindsay noticed, the door at the base of the tower began to swing slowly shut. The girl became aware of this too; she turned, made a little movement as if she would run to stop it, realized that she was too late, and stood watching it as it banged shut. She shrugged to herself, and Lindsay understood that it was a latched door—that she was locked out of the tower.

She turned back to her car, unfastened the tonneau cover and slipped a hand under it. Lindsay could not see what it was that she took out: something small, he judged by the pose of her body, but something not too easy to handle. He might have caught sight of it at the moment she refastened the cover except that, as she did so, she glanced up directly towards him and he had to jerk his head back for fear she should see him spying on her. When he dared move again it was to catch the merest glimpse of her hair as she passed right under the window. Somewhere beneath him he heard a door slam. At once he understood. The door to the tower had latched itself

against her; so she was going to use this one, just to his left at
the end of the passage.

Already, he was slightly appalled to find, he took it for
granted that he must hide; this implied so many things that
his brain reeled a little. He was eaten up with curiosity to know
who and what she was, what relation she bore to Philippe,
what it was that she carried; also implicit was the fact that they
must not meet face to face like ordinary people, both guests in
the same house, but that she had something to hide and that it
was to his advantage to find out what it was. All this he realized
in a fraction of a second, and it made him grimace to himself.
Who could argue that places, that inanimate stones and wood
did not dictate methods of behavior? As he hid himself behind
the heavy velvet curtain at the side of the window embrasure
he realized that Bellac had got him firmly by the scruff of the
neck. At Bellac this sort of behavior was normal; it had been
for hundreds of years.

He heard the girl come through the door at the far end of
the passage; he was delighted to realize from the rhythm of her
step that she was moving cautiously. He had been right to hide;
he was sure now that she did not wish to meet anyone.

He waited until she had just passed his hiding place; then
he looked out. He caught a glimpse of her face, seeming almost
shockingly close to him. The features were interesting rather
than beautiful, the nose a little too long, the chin not quite
definite enough; he thought that there had been a suggestion
of remarkable, high cheekbones and of very strong brows over
dark eyes, but he had not really seen the eyes. In any case he
had been more eager to find out what it was that she carried
—something covered with a handkerchief.

She had reached the door at the end of the passage before
the full impact of it hit him. By that time she had pulled a key
from her pocket and was fitting it into the lock. A moment
later she had gone, closing the door behind her—had gone into
the tower, carrying with great care the body of the white dove,
still transfixed by the arrow.

4

The Black Boy

They reined their horses in at the top of the bluff that over-looked the lake. It was another somber day, but between the vast cloud bastions there were glimpses of clear blue. Patterns of sunlight slid across the valley below them; a group of trees, a terraced vineyard, a solitary house, or sometimes the great brooding mass of the chateau itself was dramatically lit for a moment.

Lindsay turned from the view and looked at Philippe de Montfaucon. There was an odd contrast between the splendor of the valley laid out at their feet and the face of the man to whom it belonged. For a time, riding in the freshness of the morning, they had talked lightly, with laughter even, of the old days in Paris, the absurdities of their youth; but for the last ten minutes they had been silent; the silence had indicated, as it always had in Philippe, a change of mood. He was gazing at his domain as if it hurt him; after a moment, aware of Lindsay's eyes on him, he turned.

'I love it,' he said. 'Isn't that strange? Remember how I used to mock it?'

Lindsay nodded.

'I think that perhaps I knew all the time, at the back of my mind . . .'

'Knew?'

'That my destiny lay here.'

Destiny, thought Lindsay, was an odd word to use, surely. And yet it had been chosen with care. Philippe had always been a little pedantic in this respect; he had a regard for the French language.

'I spent a lot of time here as a child; it was a wonderful place to be a child in. Wonderful. Then, later . . . One gets very provincial in one's teens, don't you think? I suppose it's the desire to seem smart, up-to-the-minute. I grew to think of Bellac as the absolute back of beyond—a sort of Siberia; and yet ... it was *there*, James. It was in me. Do you understand that? It was waiting for me.'

'What happened? What *did* make you give up that life?'

'That life!' He threw back his head and laughed; it made him look ten years younger. 'Dear God, what Scottish censure do I detect in the phrase?'

'None. Scottish envy more like.'

He was serious again suddenly. 'Never envy those people, James. Living the way we did: a month here, three months there—Rome, New York, Lisbon, London, Rio—it's like ... like a chain of caves; one progresses ever deeper into absolute nothingness, absolute darkness, a kind of living extinction. You can see it in their faces.'

He turned his horse away from the valley, and together they rode slowly towards the terraced vineyards above them. Again Philippe was silent. Lindsay was thinking, How simple and delightful it would be if, during this ride, he would tell me everything that is at fault here. He had a sudden quixotic vision of James Lindsay, the healer, driving away up the valley in his hired Renault, leaving behind him peace where there had been discord, laughter where there had been fear. He realized that he would like to do this very much. He had spent a somewhat restless night, tormented by the mental picture of Françoise and Philippe and their delightful children. It had seemed to him almost impossible that he had come to Bellac in the faint but regrettably definite hope that in being nearer to Françoise physically he might find a way of getting nearer to her emotionally; for this he now felt ashamed of himself. At this moment—and he knew that it was a mood that would change as surely as any other—what he wanted most in the world was to see that handsome and charming family group made reality instead of the almost chilling pretense, beautifully performed withal, that he knew it to be. And so, riding slowly towards the vineyards with Philippe, he found himself thinking how satisfactory it would be if, here and now, he might be made Father Confessor to the whole complicated business.

The irony of the situation was that in a sense what he wished was coming true; on this somber morning he would hold all the clues in his hand, but he would not be able to recognize them.

The silence continued, and Lindsay fell to thinking of the explosive possibilities of words. Supposing he were to turn now and say to Philippe, 'Why haven't you slept with your beautiful wife for three years?' or 'You know, I suppose, that Françoise has a lover,' or even 'Philippe, please tell me: what was that girl doing in your tower with a dead dove?' The stupid thing was that a child could say those things and, in all probability, triumph through the direct, devastating approach; woolly adults, lost in conventional mazes of their own making, must remain silent, waiting for things to work themselves out —missing chances, wasting time, and, in the end, probably making a mess of the whole thing.

Philippe said, 'One day—it doesn't seem like seven years ago —I went along to the family lawyer for the usual annual session of total boredom; all I was interested in was the amount of money I could expect from the estates—we'd planned a rather expensive trip to India and Japan. I remember being extremely irritated because there wasn't as much as I'd expected. And then the old boy said ... Do you know it's as clear to me as if he'd said it this morning? He said, "But, Monsieur le Marquis, they've had another bad year down there!" ' He shook his head bemusedly. 'Nothing very striking in that, you might say—just a dozen ordinary words strung together. But they brought the whole of my world tumbling down round my head. I stood there, staring at him like a witless idiot. Then I turned and ran out of his office.'

They rode in silence for a few moments. Sunlight fled over them and dropped away into the valley.

Philippe said, 'It was that use of the word *another*. Do you know I suddenly felt ... a panic, James. I suddenly felt, "I must go to them." In my mind's eye I saw the whole valley, more than that, the whole estate—and all the people in it were looking towards me. I couldn't wait to get down here. I rushed back to Françoise. She was in her bath, I remember; she must have thought I was mad. I said, "Françoise, things are in a mess at Bellac, I must go down there." I got out the Bentley we used to have then—it was five o'clock in the afternoon—and I started off. I didn't stop at all; it took me nine hours. I didn't even think of letting anyone at the chateau know that I was on my way.'

He laughed again, reliving, Lindsay realized, the strange exhilaration of that night.

'I got here at two in the morning. I stopped the car at the head of the valley . . .'

Lindsay thought, In exactly the same place that I did.

'It was summer, James. Very warm, very still. I stood there looking at it in the moonlight, listening to the owls, and a dog barking miles away, and the ducks on the lake making a fuss about something. And do you know . . . I could feel . . . I could *feel* all those wasted years peeling off me.'

He had reined in his horse and was staring at the vineyards, which were golden suddenly in one of those dramatic flashes of sunlight; Lindsay, glancing at him, realized that he was not seeing anything but the wide valley under the moon, not hearing anything but the owls, and the night wind in the pines, and the noise of the ducks, alarmed by a fox perhaps.

'I got a rug out of the car and rolled myself up in it. I lay down on the grass. I felt . . . I felt suddenly that I had become myself.' He shrugged; to him it was as simple as that.

'And the people here? They were pleased to see you? After all that time?'

Philippe said, 'They . . . expected to see me.'

'Expected!'

He turned, and Lindsay was astonished by his expression —perhaps even shocked. The whole face seemed to have changed; for a moment it was almost crafty, and the dark eyes were burning with an extraordinary inner light. In spite of himself Lindsay felt a moment's . . . yes, fear. And with the fear came a sudden burst of excitement; he was absolutely and positively sure that he stood on the brink of complete understanding—that this man stood on the brink of complete explanation. But the moment died; that strange light faded out of Philippe de Montfaucon's eyes, and the moment died with it. His voice when he spoke again was colorless. 'Things were in an appalling state. It was very hard work; it took three years to get the place back on its feet, but I managed it.'

They had reached the vineyards. 'And now,' he said. 'Now...'

The whole timbre of his voice had changed. Where, a moment ago, Lindsay had heard a true note of ecstasy, he now recognized, and just as surely, the tones of despair, abject despair. Surprised, he turned to look at the man beside him, and, as he did so, he again smelled that elusive scent which had bothered him as he drove down into the valley the day before.

'Now?' he questioned, but already he thought that he knew the answer.

Philippe was staring at the vines, tier upon tier of golden vines mounting to the skyline. 'Rotten,' he said. 'There won't be a bunch of grapes, not one single bunch, worth picking.'

Lindsay, shocked, looked along the miles of vineyard and, turning, at the massed terraces on the other side of the valley.

The other man followed his eyes. 'Yes,' he said, 'all of it. Don't ask me why, I don't know. The experts don't know. They've proved that very conclusively. They came down last year in their hordes, and the advice they gave, at a price, would fill a library. Every single vine ...' His voice was rising out of despair into a tight, ugly anger. 'Every single vine was treated. Treated! God, we handled them like thousand upon thousand of expectant mothers; I shan't tell you what it cost me—it makes me retch to speak the figure. And *now* ...'

Lindsay was so appalled that he hazarded the question: 'Was it ... well, as bad last year?'

Philippe de Montfaucon looked at him then—a look of such blank purposeful despair that he should not, had he really thought about it, have been surprised at anything else, however fantastic, that was to happen. The voice had sunk to flat bitterness again. 'Last year,' he said, '*and* the year before. Not only the vines; the corn too. They've lived on potatoes.' He bowed his head and, for what seemed a long time, was lost in contemplation of his saddle. 'One comes at last,' he said finally, 'to an acknowledgment of one's responsibilities.'

And this, on looking back, James Lindsay was to remember to his dying day.

They rode back into the valley in silence. A group of laborers sitting by the side of the track touched their straw hats in deference as Philippe de Montfaucon rode by; he acknowledged their salute with an absent-minded wave of the hand. Out of the corner of his eye Lindsay thought he saw one of them raise his mug of wine to their passing. Curious, he turned, to find that they had all of them imitated this movement. They drank to their lord's health; he thought it a pretty gesture of respect, of solidarity, in view of what Philippe had told him, in the face of disaster.

They met also a man on a horse, who was presumably some kind of factor. Philippe said, 'I've been up on La Bosse. The whole lot will have to go; there's no point in pretending they won't.'

The man nodded grimly and pushed his hat onto the back of his head. 'Everyone knows how hard you tried, M. le Marquis; there's nothing but loyalty.'

Philippe nodded, withdrawn. 'The point is, Must we replant? Is this something in the vines themselves?'

'Only you will know that answer, M. le Marquis.'

Lindsay wondered a little at this reply, but Philippe did not appear to find it surprising. He smiled and looked up, meeting the man's eyes. 'Do they say that I know the answer?'

'Yes. All say it.'

Philippe nodded again. The conversation was over. The man tilted his hat forward again and rode on—not without darting a quick, appraising look at Lindsay.

After a moment he said, 'They must think you're a magician.'

Philippe laughed. 'Oh yes, they do.'

Then, changing the subject abruptly—typically: 'Tell me about your painting. Do you make money?'

Knowing that he had been politely side-tracked and curious because of it, Lindsay found himself describing his life in London. He was aware of the fact that Philippe de Montfaucon was not in any case listening to him; he looked suddenly exhausted, pale, almost as if he were finding it hard to stay in the saddle.

Lindsay knew how unpopular any reference he might make to this would be; sickness, in other people no less than in himself, had always been something that this man would never discuss. And now, for the first time, Lindsay found himself wondering why; found himself once again considering the thing that he had said to Françoise the previous evening. Perhaps, indeed, her husband was a sick man; perhaps the kindly family doctor, of whom she had spoken, had merely been telling her what Philippe wanted her to hear—husbands had hidden their own mortal illness from wives before. But in that case he would surely have invented some excuses for her before abandoning her bed, and not only her bed but her room; and sickness could not explain what she had called his 'interior withdrawal' from her. Lindsay himself had seen the dead face of disinterest, almost of dislike, that he had turned to her over the heads of their children. Again the edge of that question grated against his brain: What had she done to make him like this? He had thought it disloyal and unfair, but was it? Husbands and wives could do things to each other without being aware of what they did.

He was still asking himself questions as they rode over the drawbridge and under the echoing gatehouse into the beautiful, tree-lined Cour d'Honneur.

The boy, Christian, was sitting on the edge of the fountain that occupied the center of the courtyard; quite evidently he was waiting for them, and he made no pretense of his waiting, but simply sat, relaxed, watching them approach. Only when a groom ran forward to take the horse did he move. He came abreast of the riders a moment after the groom, who was already reaching for the reins of both mounts; but the young man stretched out his hand, and Lindsay noticed that the groom jumped back almost as if he had been slapped. Christian took the reins of Philippe's horse and held the animal while he dismounted; the groom, having apparently recovered from whatever it was that had so disconcerted him, took over from Lindsay.

It had been a curious incident. Indeed it was still curious, for the groom stood there, not looking up, waiting, until Christian turned and held out the reins to him.

But Philippe was laughing now, and the color had returned to his face; he threw an arm round the young man's shoulder and then rumpled the black hair. The boy looked up, laughing also.

It was the first time that Lindsay had seen them together; he had not expected this degree of intimacy between them.

As if aware of his eyes on them Philippe took his arm away from the young man's shoulders, but the gesture had been made —and made, Lindsay realized a little too late, intentionally. He found himself looking into Philippe's eyes, and they were darkly serious, perhaps a trifle mocking; they said, as clearly as if he had spoken the words, 'Very well, so you are curious.'

Lindsay was sure that nothing except the incident that he had just witnessed, with all its implications, would have caused him actually to *want* to sit next to the Comtesse de Vignon at luncheon. Françoise, when he asked her to see that this happened, gave him one of her dark stares, only a little disconcerted. 'You had an interesting ride, I hope,' was all she said.

'Yes, very.' He was surprised to find that he felt noncommittal; he certainly had no intention of discussing his morning with her in front of other people; deeper than this, however, he discovered that he already felt in some way disloyal to Philippe. He found himself studying the composure, which Françoise wore as a mask, with interest; he was beginning to see that this whole matter was a question of masks, though he could not say, in spite of his curiosity, that he was looking forward to that merry midnight when the masks were removed, revealing the true faces beneath.

He had a suspicion of what Philippe might be concealing. About Françoise, because she was a woman, he was a good deal less sure; but he had once known her very well, and he knew that she was concealing *something*. Moreover, because she was supposed to have enlisted his aid, he resented this state of affairs.

The Countess Betty, having spent her entire morning among horses and men who cared only about horses, was in an excellent mood; her voice resounded about the small salon in which they were taking their preprandial apéritifs. She had fixed herself to one of the two new guests, a tall, handsome and distinguished gentleman with gray, curling hair. She was saying, 'It's no good, you mustn't be cross with me, but the whole idea of hunting in Italy simply strikes me as funny. I mean do you have *foxes*, for a start . . . ?'

Françoise said sotto voce, 'Prince Rinaldo Cottanero, since you're so interested.'

Lindsay said, 'Indeed, yes; I've never moved in such circles. His lady friend is decorative.'

'She is . . . was a model—one of the top ones. He usually has models.'

Lindsay said, 'I wonder why. I understand they're extremely bad value—not that I'm an expert on the haute monde.'

'You may be,' Françoise replied at her flattest, 'before you leave Bellac. Her name is Natasha; it's a pity but she's Swiss.'

Just as they were going in to luncheon Tante Estelle arrived, looking, today, like a beige moth and holding in one hand a piece of tapestry work, in the other a silver pomander which she was pressing to the end of her long nose as if she expected the whole company to offend it.

Françoise swore competently under her breath. Tante Estelle, as if in answer, said, 'I know, I know, my dear: I never sent word. But you know I can't resist new faces.'

There was hiatus while another place was laid. As the table

was round, this involved the moving of every piece of silver and crystal upon it. Meanwhile Tante Estelle and Lindsay were introduced to the prince and his decorative friend. Lindsay decided that her eyes were just alive, even though her facial muscles were dead; he found later that she had a small, sweet, child's smile of which she seemed to be ashamed. She never spoke unless the operation was imperative.

Tante Estelle gazed at her for a moment and then said, 'You really are extremely lovely—what a strain it must be. Smell this.' And, tangentwise as ever, she shot the pomander out under Lindsay's nose.

'Mothballs,' he said, surprised.

'Camphor, child; I have a touch of sinus; the doctor says it's useless, but I disagree. I shall put it on the mantelpiece so as not to spoil the flavor of the salmon trout which I know we're going to have because I sent Marianne down to the kitchen to find out.'

Thereupon they sat down at the reorganized table. Of the people that Lindsay knew to be in the castle—and he was never exactly sure of the number the whole time he was there—only Philippe and the boy, Christian, were missing. Nobody, for one reason or another, mentioned either of them.

The Comtesse de Vignon, separated from Prince Cottanero, rediscovered Lindsay by her side. 'Ah,' she said, 'the painter!' While she was laughing at this—which was apparently, as far as she was concerned, a merry quip—Lindsay found time to wonder how her husband, that spare, rather saintly looking man who spent his life among the lepers in Africa, and of whom one occasionally caught a glimpse in a newsreel, had ever come to marry her. There could never even have been prettiness, and she was, he thought, the last type of Englishwoman that a Frenchman would find attractive. The laughter over, she was now saying, 'Marvelous stable young Philippe keeps here. If you've an eye for beauty you'd better go and take a look.'

Ten minutes of this, to Lindsay, stultifying subject led him to the loophole for which he had been looking. She said finally,

'Well, I'll tell you, I thought I had some damn fine horses, but Bellac's been an eye-opener to me.'

Lindsay said, 'Oh, you haven't stayed here before then?'

'No, this is my first visit.'

'Your son's too?'

'Well, of course; I said it's my first visit, didn't I? Marvelous fish, Françoise. Local?'

Lindsay was aware of his hostess's eye fixed on him while she explained how and where the salmon trout had been caught; he avoided it.

'Mind you,' added the Comtesse de Vignon, with her mouth full, 'God knows how one is supposed to keep track of the young these days, let alone bring 'em up.'

'Christian travels about a good bit?'

'Never stops. Good thing, I say—broadens the mind, don't you think?'

Lindsay nodded, occupied with his own thoughts. On his left Natasha sat in contented silence stuffing enormous quantities of excellent food into her exquisite figure. He spoke to her now and again—eight times, to be precise, during the meal; for reply he received five affirmatives and three negatives. There was plenty of time to devote himself to his study of Christian —too much, indeed, for what the boy's mother had to tell. Yet a picture did form itself: a large, rather lackadaisical chateau on the upper reaches of the Seine where life was centered on the stables in which the redoubtable countess raised and trained some of the finest hunting and racing horseflesh in the whole of France. In this house the great festivals of the year were the big race meetings, both French and English; the Comtesse de Vignon was one of those international figures who are never absent from the inner circles of any gathering of the turf. It was clear that her son, much to her chagrin, had other interests—declined to accompany her on her travels even when the Sorbonne gave him leisure to do so.

Lindsay was so absorbed in all this—so fascinated to find how perfectly what she was telling him complemented his preconceptions about Christian—that it was nearly the end of the meal before, in turning to address one of his token remarks to the delicious Natasha, he became aware of Tante Estelle regarding him with a good deal more than her customary birdlike interest. Having caught his eye, she favored him with one of those conspiratorial smiles. He glanced away quickly; he did not trust Tante Estelle.

He concentrated on the general topic of discussion, which appeared to be some local fete or saint's day which was soon to be celebrated, with the usual rustic junketing. A few minutes later they rose from table in a disorder of polite chatter.

Back in the little salon Lindsay found himself staring out of the window, deep in his thoughts. Françoise was pouring coffee. Madame the Comtesse Betty had again seized Prince Cottanero while his lady friend stood alone in the middle of the room, beautifully posed, staring into space.

Tante Estelle appeared at Lindsay's elbow.

'You were right,' she said suddenly, making him jump. He turned, staring at her. Evidently his obtuseness irritated her; she scowled at him. 'About the boy, about that black boy.'

Abandoning a startled vision of some young Negro, Lindsay jumped back to the present with the realization that she was talking about Christian.

'That wicked, black boy.'

'Wicked?'

They were very close to each other. The smell of the pomander with its load of camphor warred with what he took to be Chanel's Cuir de Russie.

'I said wicked. I meant it.'

Her eyes really did look quite crazy, but then, as he knew only too well, most people's eyes looked crazy in absolute proximity.

'I'm right,' he said, 'about Christian?'

'*She's* never been here before, but *he* has. In secret, you see. In secret.'

Some part of Lindsay's mind registered the fact that he was really quite afraid of Tante Estelle. But to find his suspicion so immediately, and so venomously, proved correct was a much more interesting experience.

Evidently she took his silence for some kind of doubt. 'You think that because I never go out of the house ... Oh yes, except to take tea on the lawn.' She snorted contemptuously at this particular pastime. 'You think I don't see and know.'

'Not at all,' said Lindsay. It was, indeed, the last thing he had been thinking.

'Well,' said Aunt Estelle, 'I *do* see and know.' She came a little closer. 'I hear things. *And* I have a pair of binoculars— does that surprise you?'

'Not in the least,' replied Lindsay, quite truthfully.

'What's more,' she said, 'he knows that I know. Oh yes, he knows, the wicked child.'

There flashed through Lindsay's mind a picture of the young man's face, rather beautiful in anger, as he leaned across to say to this old woman, 'Mlle. de Montfaucon does not like young people.' And what was it she had replied? 'Oh, but you are wrong. I am very fond of *young* people.' Yes, he remembered that odd accent on the word *young*.

Tante Estelle was peering into his face, trying to read what was there. He turned, and for an instant they looked at each other very closely again.

The faded eyes wavered. Surprisingly she bit her lip.

'No,' she said. 'No, no. You must be very careful. It would be better, I think, if you went back to Paris.'

Then she turned and hurried out of the room.

5

The Praying Man

He found Françoise reclining on a chaise longue in her own blue-and-gold sitting room. She had a large pair of horn-rimmed glasses balanced on the end of her pretty nose and she was reading *Figaro*. She glanced up as he came in and said, 'Ah!'

Lindsay looked at her gloomily. 'What does that mean?'

'I was expecting you.'

He sagged into a capacious wingbacked chair facing her. They regarded each other in silence for quite a long time.

'All right,' he said at last, 'so you know exactly what I've been thinking.'

Françoise nodded. 'Tante Estelle isn't the only one who can carry on a conversation and listen to somebody else's.'

Again they were silent. The buhl clock on the mantelpiece struck four times: a hurried, harassed chime as if to remind them that Time was not on their side.

Lindsay said, 'It's so damn quiet here; how do you stand it?'

'Isn't it obvious,' she said, 'that I don't?' She put down the newspaper and picked up an enormous piece of gros point. 'It's not what it seems,' she added. 'The silence, I mean. There's always a great deal going on. Perhaps these extremely thick walls have something to do with it.'

'Perhaps.'

She looked up from threading a piece of scarlet wool into her needle, and again their eyes met.

'I must say,' he burst out, 'I think you might . . .'

'James!' Her voice overrode his. 'This is going to be difficult enough for both of us without you shouting at me.'

'All right, all right.' He stood up nervously and went over to the window, looking out but not seeing anything. 'All the same, I do think you might have saved me a lot of trouble, yes and worry, if you'd told me right away what you thought—what you knew.'

'I'm not sure what I know.'

'No?' He turned on her almost brutally. 'When I asked you in Paris whether he was in love with another woman, you said, 'No, I'm sure he isn't.' You could have added that you were just as sure that he was in love with a young man. Good God, there's nothing unusual about it.'

Immediately, of course, he was ashamed of the brutality; as soon as he had given vent to the rancor—and he was sincerely annoyed with her for saying so little—it was as if the rancor had never existed.

Françoise sighed. 'I wanted someone, someone from outside, someone I could trust, to come to a conclusion; I said nothing of what I thought because I didn't want you to be influenced by other opinions.'

'Of course, of course. I'm sorry.'

'I suppose I guess correctly what that naughty old Estelle was hissing at you after lunch.'

Lindsay gave a mirthless snort of mirth. 'It was all about the boy having stayed here before.'

'Yes. While I was away.'

'How did you find out then?'

She gave him a quick look. 'Oh, there are ways.'

'Tante Estelle didn't tell you.'

'Good heavens, no; she'd be afraid to.'

'Afraid! Who of? Not Philippe.'

'And why not Philippe, may I ask?'

He stared at her.

'Oh yes,' Françoise said. 'She's afraid of Philippe all right. I don't know why, but she is.'

There was no sound for a time except the pluck of her needle through the thick canvas of the tapestry.

Eventually Lindsay said, 'He's a very odd young man, is Christian—in more ways than one.' He told her about the shooting of the dove and was slightly appalled when she expressed no surprise.

'Nothing,' she added, 'would surprise me about him—he has such ugly hands. And then his father's a saint. That must be extremely difficult.'

'You're taking it all very calmly,' said Lindsay.

'Yes, I am, aren't I? *Now.*'

She was again silent; after a moment or two he became aware of a quality in her silence. He looked at her. 'And?'

'And,' she said, 'it isn't as simple as that.'

'Isn't it?'

'Definitely no.' She spoke with such finality that he forgot his own point of view for a moment and was impressed.

'I hope,' he said, 'that we aren't going to attempt any amateur psychiatric probings into the matter; we aren't either of us equipped to do so.'

'We both of us know Philippe extremely well.'

Lindsay grunted. 'I thought I did.'

'You,' said Françoise, not deflected by this, 'shared an apartment with him for ... what? Nearly two years, wasn't it?'

'Yes, I did.' He turned to stare at her. 'Yes, I did, didn't I?' He was lost in thought suddenly, throwing his mind back across the years.

'He had,' said Françoise over her stitching, 'an affair with the girl who danced at that terrible place in Montparnasse.'

'It didn't last long.'

'Then there was Annabel.'

'Oh God,' said Lindsay, remembering that beautiful but totally empty American head, 'there was Annabel, all right. And then Martine. Martine was a very spry girl; I thought she'd marry him.'

Françoise nodded. 'And there were others. He told me— the usual premarital confession.' She looked up at him, her brows raised in a mute question above the absurd spectacles.

He shook his head. 'No,' he said, still thinking back. 'No, I'm damn sure there was nothing ... nothing else. I'd have known; good God, of course I'd have known. I mean that fellow upstairs ... what was his name? Gregoire. He and his Italian boy friend were in and out of the place all the time, borrowing things and generally raising hell. If there'd been anything, they'd have been onto it like a couple of blood-hounds. No.'

'You see,' she said, 'it's not simple, is it? Men don't suddenly ... change—for no reason.'

'No, not generally.'

She repeated, 'For no reason.'

He watched her for a while in silence. The delicate fingers moved expertly over the tapestry. He thought, with a pang of tenderness, She's had a lot of time to become expert.

'Also,' she said, 'nothing in this explains the fact that he is afraid he is going to die—soon.'

Lindsay went across the room to her and stood looking down at her fingers as if fascinated by them. 'I've got to know something,' he said at length. She nodded, and sighed. He sat down at the foot of the chaise longue watching her face and her swift fingers. After what seemed a long time she put down the work, took off her glasses and lay back, regarding him with those very brown, very bright eyes. 'No,' she said. 'I don't love him any more, not in the way you mean.' She shook her head almost wonderingly. 'I sometimes think that violent physical love—and that's what ours was, violent—comes at one moment to a point where it . . . it has to change into something else. I don't quite mean that either; I mean that it needs . . . What do they call it with these wretched rockets they're firing all over the place?'

'A booster,' Lindsay suggested.

'Yes. And it needs to find a new dimension too, a new depth. Is that it, James? Love has to keep finding new dimensions or it dies. A marriage isn't only a very special love affair, though it seems like it for a time. I think most affairs end when this point comes; either there isn't any depth, or the people concerned aren't interested in finding it.' She lay back and closed her eyes. 'Our love, Philippe's and mine, had just reached that point—it needed the booster; it needed the new dimension. And instead . . . there was this. Nothing.'

Lindsay did not speak, and she sighed deeply.

'Love died then,' she said. 'It took . . . months, years perhaps, and it was painful. But it died.' She opened her eyes again. 'But I do love him, as I love my children—do you understand that?'

'Yes. I suppose in a way I love him too.'

'Of course. That's the other reason that I wanted you . . . you, James, to come down here and help me.'

'Help you!'

'I don't want him to die.'

Lindsay was on his feet suddenly; he began to stride about the room, touching things. She watched him for a moment, then lifted her legs off the chaise longue and stood up also. He was gazing into the face of the buhl clock as if willing it to smile at him. Françoise went across to him and he turned, surprised; she stood in front of him, her eyes dark and brilliant and mysterious. Presently he put his arms round her and kissed her, hesitantly at first and then with growing passion. She realized, because of the quality of the passion, that he was angry, and she thrust him away.

'And what's that?' he demanded furiously. 'A bribe?'

Françoise slapped his face very hard indeed.

They stood there, glaring at each other, both flushed, both tensed, like a couple of animals.

'All right,' he said at last. 'Perhaps we'll get it quite straight, Mme. la Marquise.' He managed to catch her arm as it came up again, and, but less expertly, he warded off the other hand which was about to scratch his face. He held her firmly, her wrists seeming as frail as a child's against the palms of his hands. 'I want you,' he said. 'I wanted to marry you once before, and I want to marry you now, but I'm not so sure ...' He put his face nearer to hers. '... that I want to help you save your husband's life—if, as you seem to believe, it's in any danger. Do you see what I mean?'

Icy now, Françoise said, 'Very clearly. I'm surprised I ever thought you civilized.'

'Fine!' He shook her slightly, firmly. 'Well, I'm not. I'm not French either, remember that. I'm one of your uncouth allies from over the Border, and we never have liked people who try to bribe us.'

'Let go. You're hurting me.'

'You deserve to be hurt.'

Before she had time to escape him he clapped his arms round her and kissed her again. For a moment she tried to avoid his lips, but then, quite suddenly, she gave way to them; and, a second later, she bit him hard. He released her, swearing. The hand which he removed from his mouth was bloody. He turned away to the window, pulled a handkerchief from his pocket and held it to his lip.

Behind him he heard her footsteps receding; a door opened —and closed. There was finality in the sound of its closing.

Well, he thought bitterly, that's that. He knew a little about his temper; he knew where it had come from, too: his mother, a Highlander and proud of it. What was it about lips and ears that made them bleed so prodigiously? His handkerchief made him think of the white dove, and the thought of that plump body with the arrow through it made him think of Françoise, only a moment ago saying, 'It isn't as simple as that.' Suddenly, as if a shutter had lifted in his brain, he caught a glimpse of the truth—so brief a glimpse that he could not quite recognize what it was, except that it involved the dove and the girl with the helmet of golden hair, and the boy, Christian, with his different-colored eyes ... and the death, or the possible death, of Philippe de Montfaucon.

Blinded by his vision, he wheeled round, his mouth open as if to cry out. And he came face to face with Françoise.

He had not heard her come back into the room, but there she stood, a few feet from him, a dark green bottle in one hand, a piece of cotton-wool in the other, and the most enigmatic smile on her face that it had ever been his lot to witness.

He offered her his bleeding lip without saying anything; she swabbed it in silence. The impatient clock struck the half-hour.

When she had finished, he took her hand, raised it to his lips and kissed it lightly, leaving a tiny stain of blood on its whiteness. Françoise wiped off the blood with the piece of cotton-wool. Lindsay went and looked at himself in the mirror which hung behind the clock.

'How the hell am I going to explain it?'

'I think you'd better have a headache and dinner in your room; the swelling will be gone by tomorrow morning if you use plenty of this.'

He turned back to her. 'Who's the fair girl who drives the Mercedes?'

Françoise looked slightly surprised. 'Cousin Odile. You've met her?'

'I've seen her. Whose cousin?'

'Philippe's. What was she doing?'

'Now that,' Lindsay said, 'is a damned odd question.'

Françoise nodded, her eyes very serious. 'Yes, isn't it? For a damned odd girl.'

'Does she spend a lot of time here?'

'More than one suspects, I sometimes think. They don't live far away. They're a very weird family, James—one of the oldest in France, one of the most inbred: no one else being quite good enough for them.'

He was interested to observe that their passage-at-arms, whatever she might think of it privately, had brought about a change in her. The passivity that had so maddened him had vanished; her eyes were alive with intelligence and, he suspected, malice. He felt a little surge of excitement.

'Well,' he said, 'it may interest you to hear that I haven't told you the full story of that bird Christian massacred.'

'Don't tell me Odile was in on it too.'

'Oh yes.' He described how he had seen the girl take it out of her car—how he had seen her carry it into the tower. Françoise merely nodded, pursing her lips.

'And while we're on the subject,' Lindsay said, 'what about the tower? I take it to be Philippe's stronghold.'

'Yes, it is, but there's nothing surprising in that; his grandfather had it converted. It's really a sort of self-contained residence inside a residence; the old man was mad about astronomy—he had his telescope there.'

Lindsay snorted. '*You* may not find it surprising, but I do; and I find the idea of that girl retiring behind locked doors, carrying a dead bird as if it were some kind of eucharist, a lot more than surprising—I find it bloody sinister.'

Françoise stood very still for a moment, deep in thought. Then she said, 'If you asked anyone in this valley about the girl they would tell you at once that she was a witch.'

'Ah!'

'Yes, very much "Ah!" I assure you.'

'Then what's Philippe up to with her?'

'I don't know, but I'll guess. Philippe thinks he is going to die—don't ask me how or why or when or anything else about it. It doesn't even matter whether it's true at the moment. The fact is that he thinks it. He wouldn't be the first frightened man to . . . to fall back on old superstitions, would he?'

'You think she's his oracle.'

'The oracle merely foretold. I wouldn't put it past Mlle. Odile to have a try at altering the general course of things.'

Lindsay shook his head bemusedly. 'Françoise, this is the twentieth century.'

'Is it?' She looked beyond him out of the window. The enclosed valley, gray-green under rain clouds, stretched away to the mountain walls that encircled it. He could see what she meant. 'More than that,' she said. 'Is our century so robust—is our way of life so secure—are we so contented, James, that we have no need of . . . reassurance—reassurance about the things of the spirit?'

'I see what you mean. But Philippe . . .'

'Philippe is a frightened man.'

Yes, Lindsay was thinking, by God he is. He remembered that moment—only this morning—as they had ridden up from the village towards the chateau: how he had glanced at the man beside him and found him suddenly pale, suddenly crumpled, as if he barely had the strength to stay in his saddle. Yes, that could well have been fear. He had, at the time, taken it for sickness of the body, but how little different is sickness of the mind.

Françoise was watching him carefully now, probably recognizing in him the realizations which must have dawned so slowly and so painfully in her own brain.

'James,' she said, 'when you knew Philippe, did he ever go to Church?'

'No, never. Don't you remember that awful anticlerical thing he had? Practically a mania.'

'Oh yes, I remember. Supposing I told you that except for our wedding and the children's christening I've never known him to set foot in a church for three years—would you be surprised?'

'Not a bit.'

'Good. Come with me. I want to show you something.'

He could not question her further because she had already turned away. He followed her to the door and said, 'What . . . ?' But she silenced him, finger to her lips.

They went out into the corridor and along it to a narrow, arched door hidden behind a heavy curtain. Françoise took a thick, ancient key from her pocket and unlocked it; beyond was a dark stone passage, lit only by slits set in deep embrasures. Lindsay realized that they were inside the thickness of the castle walls; here, in the distant past, archers had stood to fire on an advancing enemy.

At the end of the passage was another door. Françoise stopped in front of it and turned to him. 'Now really,' she whispered, 'not a sound, James. This key is supposed to be lost.' She inserted it into the lock of the door, turned it with infinite caution and grimaced as the mechanism clicked into place. She waited then for a full minute before opening the door very slightly; she looked through the aperture, a mere two inches, nodded, and stepped back out of his way.

Lindsay was surprised to find himself gazing, from a forest of organ pipes, down the length of a very beautiful chapel—a very old chapel, too, for the arches were rounded and therefore Norman, or possibly even Roman.

Because his eye was led, as the eye always is, directly to the altar, he did not immediately see Philippe de Montfaucon —the huddled, motionless figure on its knees in the transept directly opposite the door through which he was peering.

He turned and looked at Françoise. She nodded, closed the door as gently as she had opened it, turned the key in the lock, and, without another word, led him back along the passage.

Neither of them spoke until they stood once more in the blue-and-gold elegance of her little sitting room.

'You *knew*,' Lindsay burst out. 'You were sure that he'd be there.'

'Yes.' The implications of this did not need to be spoken.

Lindsay shook his head bemusedly. '*Every* day?'

'Every day.'

'For how long?'

'An hour, two hours; the longest I ever knew was twelve.'

'Twelve!'

Her eyes were full of a kind of pain now. 'All night.'

They stared at each other, their minds trying to find a hold upon the enormous, glassy cliff of this knowledge.

'For God's sake,' Lindsay suddenly cried out, 'what's going on in this place?'

Françoise, never taking her deep eyes off him, said, 'That, James, is what I hope we're going to find out.'

6

The Fourteen Deaths

It is an unfortunate fact that a bite administered by human teeth never looks like anything but a bite administered by human teeth. There are very few ways of explaining how such a mark could have appeared on one's lip—particularly to the sort of company then assembled at Bellac. And so Lindsay lay on his bed, watching the gray day die outside the window, listening to the silence.

He realized that he was caught, held hand and foot by this castle and the mystery that it contained. The problems and the contradictions boiled inside his brain. Every now and again he would get up, prowl a few times round the room, and come to rest at the window, gazing out at the bruised purple of the mountains, the low clouds billowing in from the west, the livid crescent of the lake, reflecting suddenly a last pale relic of dead sunlight.

What particularly taunted him about the whole conundrum was a lurking suspicion at the back of his mind that he did, in fact, know the answer to it—or, more exactly, that he knew *an* answer which would in its turn release all the others, like the first log that moves with the thaw in a frozen river. And this answer, he was sure, lay in the character of Philippe de Mont-faucon—the man who had turned suddenly from his wife, who spent his days, so it seemed, closeted with either a child witch or Tante Estelle's 'black, wicked boy,' or else by himself in prayer or meditation; the man who was young, strong and healthy but who was afraid of death.

Françoise had said, 'He isn't just living at Bellac, he *is* Bellac.' Very well, the answer lay in these stones.

Lindsay pressed his hand against the cold wall of the room as if bidding it to communicate to him what it knew. Then, once more, he began to prowl; and, once again, he came to the bed and fell onto it.

Presently however he thought, Yes, I'm right: the answer lies here in the stones of Bellac. But what do I know of them? Nothing.

He began to think of the library, that magnificent but intimidating room next to the little salon in which they had lunched. Since the story of his headache had doubtless already been put about, he did not particularly want to meet any of his fellow guests face to face on the stairs; did not in any case want to give them the chance to read the evidence of his lower lip. He estimated, however, that at a certain time before dinner —say three-quarters of an hour—they would all certainly be in their rooms, dressing. At a quarter to eight, therefore, he left his bedroom and went along the passage that led to the staircase. There was no one in sight. That thick, blank silence carpeted the place. He went quickly downstairs, across the immense shadowy hall, in which a huge log fire burned even in summer, and into the library.

It took him quite a long time to find the light switches, cunningly hidden behind a piece of paneling. He was then faced with tier upon tier of books; he reasoned that there must, somewhere, be a catalogue. There were, in fact, no less than five.

Half an hour later he regained his room, having been seen by no one but a manservant and a Great Dane. He spread the spoils of the expedition on the desk in the window, switched on a reading light, and sat down. He had found *Bellac—the Unspoiled Land* by Pierre Basse, *The Castle of Bellac—Its Foundation and History* by Professor Puget, *Mediaeval Days and Ways—a Reconstruction in Four Volumes Based on the Bellac Manuscripts now in the National Library*, *Montfaucon—a History* by G. H. Latour, and *Montfaucon—a Record of Thirteen Centuries* by Gervaise de Montfaucon; he had not chosen some twenty others.

The servant who brought the patient's dinner found the latter absorbed in an immense tome. Lindsay, lost in the past, hardly noticed the succulent meal, did not even glance up when the tray was removed, and was still sitting there in a pool of light when Françoise came up to see how he was some three hours later. By this time *Montfaucon—a Record of Thirteen Centuries* was marked in a dozen places by slips of paper. The eye that Lindsay lifted to regard her was steely with excitement.

'What a family you married into,' he said.

Françoise looked at the spine of the book. 'Interesting, isn't it?'

'You've read it?'

'Some of it.'

'It strikes me,' Lindsay said, 'that your husband might well be afraid of sudden death on the basis of statistics alone. Good God, it practically runs in the family!'

'They seem to have been an unreliable collection, don't they?'

'*Un*reliable? Their wives could practically *count* on being widows before they were forty.' He picked up a piece of note-paper from the desk, the falcon crest flamboyant at the top of it, and began to read from the penciled notes he had made. 'Jehan, killed in battle, the year 960, aged thirty; Gillaume le Blanc—Why "the white," do you suppose?—murdered on the road in the year 1009. Philippe ditto in the year 1057; *he* was only twenty. Blaise, ditto but in battle. Alain, the year 1220, died while out hunting; it doesn't say how . . .'

Françoise said, 'Those were violent days, James; and remember it's rare to have a record of one family in such detail.'

Lindsay gave a sarcastic snort of mirth. 'It always *has* been violent days as far as these boys are concerned. Heavens above, what about your husband's grandfather? *He* got shot while out hunting too. If I were Philippe I'd leave blood sports strictly alone.' He stood up and began once more to pace about the room.

Françoise leaned against the door watching him. 'You think . . . You really think,' she said at length, 'that it has something to do with Philippe's fear of dying?'

'I'm damn sure it has; it's too tidy to be just coincidence. My dear Françoise, listen: there's a record here of thirty-five male Montfaucons in the past ten centuries, thirty-five heads of the family, and that's a hell of a lot in any case—and hardly any of them reigned to a ripe old age. Now, of those thirty-five we'll count out nine who died in battles of various kinds; that leaves twenty-six, doesn't it? Of those twenty-six, fourteen—more than half, Françoise—came to grief in what I can only call suspicious circumstances.' He glared at his list again as if accusing it of homicide. 'My dear girl, look at Gils here, 1422; a *tree* fell on him! I ask you!'

Françoise came into the room and sat on the edge of the bed, deep in thought.

Lindsay laughed again; he was a little drunk with excitement. 'Has he ever said anything to you about this bloodstain on the family tree?'

She shook her head. 'He's joked about it once or twice.'

'Joked! There's no accounting for tastes, is there?' He consulted his notes again, frowning. 'I suppose you could say that his father at least chose a *new* way of disposing of himself: but isn't drowning a bit odd? Where did he drown, to begin with? Not in the lake out there?'

'No, at Antibes. Nobody quite knows how it happened.'

Lindsay heaved a deep sigh and echoed her. 'Nobody quite knows how it happened. I bet the women of this family have been saying that, in just that tone of voice, all the way down the centuries. You don't suppose there's some crazy blood feud, do you? Vendetta, and all that? No, of course there isn't.'

Françoise said, 'Do you know it's past midnight? And have you been putting that stuff on your lip?'

He stood patiently while she dealt with the bruise; then, when she was turning away, he caught her hand and restrained her. 'I'm sorry,' he said, 'about this afternoon.'

For answer she reached up and kissed his cheek. 'I'm not,' was all she said. 'Good night. You don't look as though you'll go to bed for hours.'

He did not find any difficulty in going to bed, but sleep was another matter. After an hour of tossing and turning he gave up the struggle, switched on the light and reached for *Montfaucon—a History* by G. H. Latour. He was interested to find that this nineteenth-century publication seemed to make a point of *not* explaining anything at all about the deaths of the male Montfaucons, though it was true that M. Latour gave a few details about those who had actually been killed in battle —most of them fighting against whoever at that moment was generally accepted to be King of France—and he had been unable to resist the sad tale of Gils, upon whom the tree had fallen. All the others, without exception, were simply said to have died; the date was given, but no details. And in Volume Four of the Bellac Manuscripts there was a full version of the family tree, with notes; again, the Montfaucons who had died in battle were given special mention, but those who, according to *Montfaucon—a Record of Thirteen Centuries*, had been 'murdered upon the road,' or 'killed while out hunting,' or 'set upon whilst returning from the Pilgrimage' were tacitly ignored; even poor Gils, it was implied, had simply expired in bed.

This seemed to Lindsay a rather curious state of affairs, almost as if the family were being a little coy about their death rate. He lay back in the bed and gave himself up to speculation: now, supposing this were true, supposing there was some sort of conspiracy of silence—even the Record of Thirteen Centuries was far from explicit—what in the name of heaven could be the reason? It could only mean that the Montfaucon honor or pride or good name would suffer if the absolute truth were known. This surely implied something like insanity; perhaps suicide had figured a little too blatantly in those mysterious causes of death; and if indeed Philippe had suddenly turned homosexual in his twenty-ninth year after a youth spent in almost continuous pursuit of various beautiful women ... Insanity, sexual inversion, suicide: they all *had* been known to run in families ... What about Grandfather Edouard, another one killed out hunting? Indeed what about Alain, Philippe's own father, drowned while taking a swim at Cap d'Antibes? And *that*, in view of the family history, was a likely story ... And what about ... ?

He awoke with a start. Someone, holding a knife, was leaning on his chest; the dark shape of him reared up and seemed to fall on him, blotting out the ceiling of the room.

He rolled over, sweating, and turned on the light. The weight on his chest was, of course, M. Latour's fat history; the dark shape was the canopy of the fourposter. He was flooded with that warm relief which comes with the knowledge that it was all a nightmare; then, suddenly, he sat bolt upright in the bed, staring. But he had been reading when he fell asleep; he had been reading, and the light had been on!

He turned and stared at the bedside lamp. Somebody then *had* been in the room while he slept; yes, the first thing an interloper would do would be to turn out the light. He looked round, searching the shadows; he lifted up the lamp and shone it into the darker corners, revealing his shirt thrown over a chair, his painting things neatly arranged by a maidservant, his shoes in the middle of the floor.

Or had he turned the light out himself? He couldn't remember doing it, but, equally, he couldn't remember leaving his shoes in the middle of the floor; it would be impossible to deny that his mind had definitely not been on mundane objects like shoes and lights. Yes, come to think of it he had probably switched it off himself.

He was just relaxing again—just getting used to this comforting explanation—when he caught sight of the book still lying open across his body. A little frisson of fear ran down his spine.

For the book was not M. Latour's *Montfaucon—a History;* it was *The Collected Fairy Tales of Charles Perrault.*

7

The Yellow-eyed Girl

Lindsay sat in the sun, drawing. He did not feel in the mood for it, and he did not like the particular wing of the chateau which he was committing to paper, but at all times it soothed him to hold a pencil, and on this particular morning it afforded him the best possible excuse for sitting and watching. In spite of an almost totally sleepless night he felt very much alert.

So he had been warned. 'Fairy tales,' he had been told, 'are a better occupation for ignorant little boys than prying into matters which do not concern them.'

At first he had been sure that only Françoise knew that he had taken those books to his room; then he remembered the anonymous someone—it had been a man—who had brought up his dinner tray and later removed it. And the maddening thing was that he, in his total absorption, had not even looked up at the fellow's face; he felt that it would, to say the least, have been helpful to recognize him again. In the meantime he had to wait until Françoise emerged from her boudoir, which was never, as far as he could see, before midday; he knew that her children joined her there for breakfast; he also knew something of her addiction to long, hot baths—between the two, he imagined, her morning was completely occupied.

And so he sat, drawing but not thinking of drawing; he was, in fact, wondering what would happen next.

What happened next was that the boy, Christian, appeared on the terrace, saw him, and moved towards him. Lindsay was pleased; there is a sort of person who cannot resist a man with a pencil in his hand—often, but not always, they are people possessed of a certain physical beauty.

Christian smiled his good morning, leaned against the low stone wall that edged the terrace, and gazed at the chateau. 'Do you really like it?' he asked with, Lindsay thought, quite genuine astonishment. 'I think it's grisly.'

'It is rather.' He looked up at the arrogant young face with interest. It had all the bounding vigor of extreme youth—the sunlight seemed to glow out of the brown skin rather than into it; the smooth planes were unblemished, faultless; the thick, black hair, so closely cut, was as glossy as the fur of a young animal.

Clearly Christian enjoyed being scrutinized for he smiled.

'All right,' Lindsay said. 'But move a bit farther away. Sit on the wall. You'll have to keep fairly still.'

It had struck him that he could very easily anchor this boy, who was after all one of the central characters of the mystery, fast to his side with the chains of his own vanity. Besides, there was nothing like drawing a face for making one aware of its secrets, its inconsistencies. Lindsay knew that even the most faultless features, even the blankest type of young-girl beauty, revealed something strange during its transposition to a piece of paper. And this face was far from blank.

'You like it here?' he asked.

Christian smiled. 'Yes. Do you?'

'It's interesting. It's been getting steadily more interesting ever since the rather odd welcome you gave me.'

The boy said nothing.

'Do you often go about shooting tame birds with a bow and arrow?'

The strange eyes flickered over him for a moment—a look as cold, removed, disinterested as that of a parrot. 'Oh,' he said, 'I was after a crow. They've been killing the doves.'

He was so bored with his own lie—so bored, perhaps, with the necessity for having to tell one—that he did not even try to make it convincing.

'Are you such a bad shot then?'

He smiled. 'No. As a matter of fact I'm rather good.'

'Sometimes, apparently.'

The smile deepened for a moment and then withdrew.

Lindsay was having trouble with the spacing of the eyes; he was astonished to find how far apart they were.

Christian said, 'You knew Philippe during his Paris days. He must have been fun then.'

'Yes, he was. Isn't he . . . fun now?'

At this the young man threw back his head and roared with laughter. Smiling, Lindsay found himself, as he had not expected to be, in sympathy with the arrogance, with the barely veiled insolence. It was difficult, he realized, not to fall under the spell of healthy young animals who have no misconceptions about their world, but simply *know* that it belongs to them.

Serious again, Christian said, 'He's a wonderful person.'

Lindsay had discovered something odd about this face; it emerged from his first sketch of it, which was like and yet utterly unlike; was, in fact, the face of a half-wit, a mongol. Fascinated by the discovery and its implications, he did not speak for some time. Yes, it was true; the eyes *were* too widely spaced, yet in the flesh this was barely apparent. The surprising lift to the cheekbones was, in the flesh, in some way canceled out or, now that he came to look again, balanced by the boy's high color; yet in the drawing, robbed of coloring, the face that looked back at him was primitive, and the youthful yet mocking glance emerged as mere slyness.

He was fascinated; he had in front of him a rough sketch which was indubitably Christian, but Christian stripped down to the barest essentials that his face revealed. He knew that he could not touch it again; it was far too interesting as it was. He tore off the page, tucked it into the pad, and began again.

The young man, noticing the fresh start, said, 'Are you a good painter?'

It was Lindsay's turn to laugh, and his laughter was clearly not what Christian had expected. He flushed.

Lindsay decided to pounce. 'Where did you meet Philippe? I gather he never leaves this valley nowadays.'

'Oh ... he's a friend of my mother's.'

'Ah, I see. This is your first visit to Bellac—I hadn't realized that.'

Glancing up, Lindsay found the strange eyes fixed on him. The sun caught one of them, the other was in shadow; it made their difference in color even more startling. The boy said nothing.

Lindsay said, 'Well, don't glower; it makes you look positively hideous.'

Now that he knew this unexpected secret about the face, drawing it was easy. In order to capture its quality, in order to give it what it seemed to possess, it was necessary to cheat— the eyes had to be pulled closer together and the cheekbones flattened, as they were flattened in life by the high coloring. The forehead, which the young man's fashionable, Left Bank haircut tended to compress, had to be lifted to imply a brain behind it, and the melancholy—even melancholic—line of the mouth had to be raised to mimic the vigor and alertness which, although they were there in Christian, were most unwilling to emerge on paper.

Altogether, thought Lindsay, roughing in the strong shadows thrown by the sunlight, a most rewarding half-hour.

Christian said, 'You're looking very pleased with yourself.'

'You're an interesting subject.' The sketch might be finished, but he had no intention of letting the young man slip away from him forever. 'I'd like to paint you; I wonder if your mother would care to pay me.'

'She would,' said Christian, 'if I wanted her to.'

'You can show her this, and ask her.'

'Is it finished?'

'Yes, for what it is worth.'

Christian came round to look at it. He was, Lindsay realized without surprise, the kind of person who cannot stand near to anyone without touching him; he put an arm round Lindsay's shoulder. Yes, Lindsay thought, an animal. Most interesting, and far from unlikable.

Christian thought the drawing very good; Lindsay himself

was quite pleased with it—this was the first time for some weeks that he had felt the true creative tingle in his fingertips.

'Yes,' he said. 'I really would like to paint you; perhaps we'll forget Mother and simply do it for fun.'

'Good God, no!' The boy was genuinely shocked. 'It'd do her good to buy something sensible for a change instead of endless, endless successions of bloody horses.'

Studying him, Lindsay wondered, How exactly do you fit into this puzzle, young man?

They were interrupted by voices. The speed with which the young man removed his arm from Lindsay's shoulder gave the latter pause for further thought. All things, he decided, were revealing once you began to question them.

Betty, Comtesse de Vignon sailed out onto the terrace with a neigh of laughter, followed by Prince Cottanero and the beautiful Natasha. The Countess and the Prince were dressed for riding; Natasha was dressed for luncheon at the Ritz.

Christian stood, hands on hips, watching them approach; when they were near enough he said, 'Maman, Mr. Lindsay wants to paint my portrait.'

'Then he shall, my darling.' She turned to Lindsay. 'In the red shirt, don't you think? I adore him in that red shirt.' She finished by calling her son her little cuckoo, which, even in French, sounded idiotic.

Lindsay, his eyes opening wider moment by moment, thought, You stupid, stupid woman—not content with forcing him into a life of his own about which you know nothing and care less, you try and dote on him as well. In truth, parents do murder their own progeny.

'I make one condition,' she was saying to her son. (There would be a condition, Lindsay thought.) 'That you fetch your nice new camera and come and take a picture of that ravishing horse.'

Presumably Christian thought this a reasonable price to pay for the pleasure of having a portrait of himself in a red shirt. He went along like a lamb, winking at Lindsay as he did so.

Prince Cottanero seemed inclined to linger; perhaps he was tired of the Countess Betty's company.

'Would you not like to paint Natasha?' he inquired, patting her shoulder as if she were a favorite cat.

'Very much.' Lindsay had an absurd momentary vision of himself spending the rest of his life moving from chateau to castello to schloss, painting the objects-of-adoration of their owners.

Surprisingly Natasha said, 'Oh no, Rinaldo; I'm just pretty.'

Either of them, Lindsay was thinking, would make an interesting subject. The two faces of the boy, Christian, had made him feel very aware of people; he saw, for the first time, that Cottanero also was not exactly what he presented himself as being. What had at first seemed to be a face of handsome virility was in fact something else; or rather the handsome and virile face, fashionably tanned, short curly hair fashionably gray, was betrayed by the eyes—there was something evasive about the eyes, something soft, not with that melting softness which Italian eyes sometimes achieve in their rare moments of sentimentality, but soft with a softness that penetrated directly to the center of the man.

With a sense of shock, and a sense of excitement too, Lindsay thought, Heavens above, you're a fake as well.

He felt suddenly that at any moment the chateau, the bright sky, the distant mountains might give a shudder and soar upwards, revealing the brick wall of the stage behind them.

He turned and looked at Natasha; their eyes met, and in hers he caught a flash of something very different to the almost idiotic, dreaming placidity which he had always seen there before. He realized that these people were not the only ones who were revealing themselves; the growing excitement—excitement of the chase—which he felt, must have been printed all over his face. The girl turned away; she did it, he knew, to hide her eyes. An electric spark of antagonism ran about between them.

Prince Cottanero said, 'I am sorry, Mr. Lindsay, that you . . . injured your lip. Come, my dear.'

They left Lindsay hugging himself with delight. After all he *was* a Scot, and the Scots love a fight. Oh yes, he thought, the daggers are out this morning. What next?

He heard Françoise and her children long before he saw them. The voice of Gilles, the small boy, was raised in wrath, that of Antoinette in a wail of indignation; Françoise was saying, 'Gilles, for heaven's sake sit down; it'll be your turn next.'

They were sitting in the shade of a willow tree beside the lake, for the sun was by now extremely hot. Lindsay stood for a little while watching them—the play of light and shadow over them; he knew that he would not be able to say any more than Manet and Renoir had already said. All the same they made a charming picture. The small girl was acting, with enormous gravity, a scene from some story, a complicated scene; at intervals she would say, 'Now I'm the other person,' or 'Now I'm a new person.'

Gilles said, 'You're being four people already, it isn't fair.'

Lindsay waited until they had guessed—or rather failed to guess, much to Antoinette's delight—what the scene was supposed to be. He then joined them.

Gilles said, 'Were you drawing a picture of Christian?'

'Yes, I was. Did you see me?'

'Mm. Maman wouldn't let us come and watch.'

He caught Françoise eyeing him, opened his sketchbook and showed her the finished sketch.

'Oh,' she said, 'it's quite different.'

'Different?'

'To the style I used to know.'

'Well, I haven't stood still—any more than you have.'

She smiled. 'It's rather good, isn't it?'

'Why,' demanded Antoinette, gazing up into his face, 'did you draw Christian?'

'Because . . .' Again he glanced at Françoise. '. . . I was interested in his face.'

Antoinette said, 'Oh.' She clearly thought it a pretty silly answer.

Gilles said, 'Draw us.'

'You're too young,' Françoise chipped in. 'You haven't got proper faces yet.' This, very rightly, Lindsay thought, produced screams of protest.

He said, 'You go and play over there, by the boat, and I'll see what I can do.'

They removed themselves with alarming obedience, went and stood by the ancient punt which was pulled up onto the bank, and gazed at him self-consciously.

Antoinette said, 'Maman, I don't want my picture done.'

'I do,' said Gilles.

After a little while they lost interest in this game and began to play leapfrog.

Lindsay took the other drawing of Christian out of his sketchbook and put it in front of Françoise. She made rather a vulgar whistle through her teeth.

'See what I mean?'

'I don't know about that, but I see what you saw.' She laughed suddenly. 'Poor boy! He's really rather pretty, and he's far from half-witted.'

'Not far, I'd say.'

She turned, looking at him seriously. 'You believe that, don't you?'

'I've got certain theories about faces; most painters have.'

She stared at the drawing in silence for a long time. Meanwhile he drew a large number of quick cartoons of the oblivious children.

At length she said, 'In that case I'm afraid of him.'

Lindsay snorted. 'You've got a very odd lot of people here altogether.'

'You wait.'

'Not more?'

'Two more for lunch. That's only the beginning.'

'You gave me the impression that you lived like hermits.'

She sighed. 'Well, don't we—in a sense? Besides ... we always get this every year; they come down for Les Treize Jours.'

'You have this lot for thirteen days? You poor woman.'

'No, the Thirteen Days in question are ... or, rather, is one day—next Friday. Oh for heaven's sake, James, don't tell me you didn't hear them all talking about it for half lunch-time yesterday.'

'Oh, the local fete thing.'

'Yes, the local fete thing. Why it's called the Thirteen Days nobody knows, except that once upon a time it may have lasted for thirteen days. Anyway, it's always been a family tradition to have people here for it; in fact at one time there used to be a vast houseparty. Philippe's mother had to cope with it once or twice; I gather it nearly drove her mad—getting the right people next to the right people, and remembering who wasn't on speaking terms with whom, and who was sleeping with whom, and who wanted to sleep with whom. It must have been a nightmare. Thank God I've been spared it.'

'How do I get to meet Philippe's mother, Françoise? It might be interesting.'

'She died years ago; she never really got over her husband being drowned like that.'

He nodded. 'That's a pity. Aren't there any other members of ... well, the older generation we can talk to?'

'If there were, do you imagine I wouldn't have done so long ago? Tante Estelle is the only one who ... who might know a few things.'

'And she isn't easy to talk to?'

Françoise grimaced. 'She isn't even easy to *get* to. She's being very amenable at the moment because she can't resist strangers; sometimes she shuts herself up in that suite of hers and the only person she allows near her is her blessed Marianne—for weeks on end.'

Looking at her he was touched by the brooding sadness of her expression. She said, 'You may think them a rather odd lot of people, but I don't mind; they're better than nothing.' She turned, looking full at him. 'Do you know that when Philippe spoke to me on the day you arrived ... You remember?'

'I remember half-a-dozen words.'

She nodded grimly. 'It was the first time for a week—since I got back from Paris.'

'Perhaps he knows what you were doing in Paris.'

She colored slightly and looked away. 'You aren't ... kind about that.'

'I told you, I'm jealous.'

She shook her head, staring at him again; then, gently, she pushed back a lock of hair from his forehead. 'You're a child,' she said. 'You make me feel old.'

'I'm older than you are.'

'No man is older than any woman—not in that sense. When a husband tells a wife to her face that she had better go and get herself a lover, he's hardly likely to object when she takes him at his word.'

Lindsay gaped at her. 'He said that?'

'Oh yes, and more. I admit he was drunk, but ...'

'Drunk! Philippe!'

She nodded.

'Françoise, I never saw him drunk the whole time we shared that flat together.'

She spread her hands, brows raised.

'But what's making him like this?'

'Do you think I haven't asked myself that a thousand times?' She began to pull up stalks of grass, almost viciously.

Lindsay said, 'He's terribly worried about this blight on the vines, isn't he?'

'How would I know? He never talks to me.' The sadness in her voice caught at his heart.

After a moment he said, 'Marry me, Françoise.'

'I am married.'

'Divorce him.'

'I'm a Catholic.'

'Divorce him all the same. Before he destroys you. If your faith forbids it, under these circumstances, it's high time ...'

'I'm sorry. I admit I was hiding behind my faith, James. Yes, if—don't be angry—if my conscience would let me, I'd divorce him.' She went on quickly before he could remonstrate. 'But I believe, still, that I can help him.' She leaned forward, pressing his hand, urging him to see this devious path of duty which was so very clear to her. 'I believe he needs help—desperately; he needs friends. We can help him, James. We must help him.'

Bitterly he said, 'You think he needs *us*?'

'Yes. He may not know it, but he does. I know . . . I *know*, my dear, that the moment will come when he'll turn away from . . . from whatever it is that possesses him. At that moment—at that one moment—he will need help.'

He would remember, later, every word of this; it was as if her passionate conviction could, in some way, stamp itself upon the future—bend the future to conform with what she so desperately believed. Sitting there beside the lake, her hand gripping his, she had spoken a prophecy—half a prophecy.

Lindsay, being a man, was too full of himself to accept any of it; he would have said that he saw things straighter than she did, forgetting that life is never straight. He was remembering, too, with irritation, that he had wanted to tell her about his experience of the previous night, of the warning laid upon his sleeping chest in the shape of a book of fairy stories. After the passion of her outburst he did not now see that he could work the conversation back to anything so mundane without seeming a callous lout.

He was still wrestling with this problem, and she was still pressing his hand, staring into his sulky face, when they heard the unmistakable roar of the Mercedes.

Françoise turned her head sharply. 'She's stopping.'

They both looked up at the road, which at this point followed the curve of the lake, divided from it by only a narrow field. The white car was driving slowly round the bend, and the face of the girl at the wheel was turned towards them, very dark glasses masking her eyes. The brilliant hair shone in the sunlight.

'She *is* stopping.'

Lindsay was shocked to recognize fear in her voice; he turned to look at her. She was staring up at the car, biting her lip.

'Steady on,' he said. 'She's not *really* a witch, you know.'

'I don't like her.'

'Evidently.'

But the white car was slowing to a standstill; it bumped onto the grass verge and came to a stop. The girl got out, waved to them, and began to climb the fence into the field.

'Now why?' said Françoise. 'Why?' She looked reflectively at her children, who were sailing the grounded punt across oceans of the imagination; then she looked at Lindsay.

'You,' she said. 'Yes, it must be something to do with you.'

'Does it have to be something to do with something? I mean, people do talk to people without motives.'

Françoise gave him one of her unfathomable looks, when the light, the life, in her eyes seemed to have withdrawn into a deep dark cave. She said nothing, but turned and watched the girl coming towards them.

To Lindsay she looked almost exactly like any one of the rather untidy maidens who slopped about St. Tropez all summer. She wore the same trousers that he had seen before and a shirt hanging outside them; her feet were bare; she was very brown. Whatever else she might be was obscured by the dark glasses.

Françoise said, 'Odile! I haven't seen you for ages. This is James Lindsay. Mlle. de Caray.'

The girl smiled at Lindsay and sat down in one movement like a cat; the fact that she settled a little way from them—that is to say, a little farther from them than was quite natural—and then in a tuft of long grass, increased her likeness to that animal.

She said, 'It's so hot; it makes me lazy.'

Lindsay felt (quite wrongly as it happened) that he was beginning to get the measure of the people who frequented Bellac; in any case she had tickled his sense of humor so that he could not help laughing. The dark glasses were leveled at him. 'You find this funny—that the heat makes me lazy?'

'No,' he said. 'It's you, mademoiselle; you are so like a cat.'

She smiled. 'How nice of you, monsieur! My mother says

that I am like a ferret. Now, I ask you, is that a nice thing to call your daughter?'

'Horrible.'

She shrugged. Clearly what her mother thought was of no interest to her.

The children had now rejoined them—Tante Estelle was not the only person at Bellac unable to resist strangers—and stood looking at Mlle. de Caray.

Gilles said, 'Show us a trick, Odile.'

'It's too hot.'

From the sudden stillness of Françoise beside him, Lindsay gathered that this was the first time she had heard of 'tricks'; a moment later she verified his suspicion by saying, 'But how interesting! What trick did Odile show you, darling?'

The small boy rubbed one leg against the back of the other. 'Oh, just tricks. You know.'

Odile, sucking a piece of grass, said, 'I turned a frog into a goldfish, didn't I, Gilles?'

Antoinette, jumping up and down, shouted, 'You didn't, you didn't! The goldfish was there all the time under the water lily.'

'No, truly,' said Gilles, 'truly, Maman, she did turn the frog into a fish. I saw.'

Antoinette chanted, 'Silly, silly, silly.'

Françoise, pulling her son towards her and hitching up his trousers, which seemed to be in danger of falling off, said, 'You've got too much imagination, that's your trouble.'

'No one,' the girl replied, 'can have too much imagination.'

'Wait until you have children.'

'Children? Me!' She really was genuinely surprised—almost, Lindsay could have sworn, affronted. 'Françoise, what do you take me for?'

Something in all this had made Françoise angry. She said, 'I take you for a child yourself—and sometimes a rather naughty one.'

Odile lay down with her cheek against the grass. Reflectively she said, 'Yes. I daresay you're right there. But, Holy Face, what would life be like with no imagination?' She rolled over and took off the dark glasses. 'Don't you think so, Mr. Lindsay?'

This was the first time that Lindsay had seen her eyes, and they took him by surprise, for they were amber, two gleaming disks of tawny amber. And *disks* was the right word, for the pupils were very little darker than the iris—there was absolutely no denying that the effect was rather uncanny. He could well understand that the local peasants might call her a witch.

'Imagination,' he said. 'I'm the wrong person to ask. I never quite know where imagination begins and reality ends.'

At this the girl sat up and looked at him; focused all of her rather remarkable personality on him. The amber eyes widened. 'Ah,' she said, 'but this is the point—how intelligent of you! There is no such thing as either reality or imagination; they are the same thing. Gilles saw me turn the frog into a goldfish; Antoinette knew that the goldfish was underneath the water lily all the time. As it happens neither of them was right, but where is the reality and where the imagined thing? Which is which?'

'This,' Lindsay said, 'makes scientists the stupidest people in the world.' He was absolutely fascinated by her eyes.

The girl spread her hands. 'Who denies that they are? Give a scientist enough time and he would arrive at what he would call the truth, which is that I had caught the goldfish before the children appeared; then I saw the frog, and I thought, Here's a chance for some magic. What's childhood without a little magic? And so I did my "trick." But the reality was not the dry truth, it was what the children saw—and what they saw, they saw with their imaginations.'

Lindsay could see, in his mind, the little cold body of the goldfish secreted in her brown hand; each golden scale was clear to him, and the magical sheen of the belly, as if it had been painted with a rainbow. And the wonderful golden eye, ringed with a circle of black. And in the golden eye of the golden fish could be seen reflected the Chateau of Bellac and the lake, and the round, surprised faces of the children—children watching a miracle in the golden eye of a goldfish. . . .

Suddenly he felt violently sick; it began with a nausea, and then gripped his stomach so that he had to fight in order not to vomit. He heard himself let out a groan. The sea of quivering gold—it was like looking out to sea directly into the eye of the sunset—receded, lapped away into illimitable distance.

Françoise said, 'James, are you all right?'

He opened and shut his eyes once or twice. 'Yes. Yes, perfectly.'

He looked up. Odile de Caray was plaiting three pieces of grass, very intent on what she was doing.

'I . . .' He shook his head again. 'I felt a bit sleepy, that's all.'

The girl smiled. 'Ah,' she said, 'so I am not the only one the heat affects in that way. Well—I'd better be going.'

She stood up, again in one sinuous movement, and put on her dark glasses. 'Nice to see you again, Françoise—and you, monsieur.'

She waved to the children, who had returned to the punt, and walked slowly away from them across the field.

Françoise said, 'James, what on earth . . . ? I thought you were going to faint.'

Lindsay, frowning at the slim retreating back, said, 'What a little bitch! She hypnotized me—just like that.'

Françoise let out a gasp.

'Just like that,' he said. 'I fell for it completely.'

'Hypnotized you!'

'There's nothing extraordinary about it. Masses of people can do it. But not as quickly as that, not as effortlessly.'

'But why? Why did she?'

'I may be wrong, but I think as a warning.' He told her then about the book of fairy tales that had taken the place of the Montfaucon history while he slept.

'Oh no,' she said. 'Oh, I don't like that at all, James.'

'I do. I like it very well.'

'But I feel . . . It was my idea that you should come here; I feel responsible for you.'

He ignored this. Eyes narrowed against the glare, he watched the girl get into her glamorous car.

'I like it,' he said, 'because it proves that we're on the right track. I must get back to my history, Françoise.'

8

The Frightened Aunt

Lindsay counted ten people, excluding himself, sipping their apéritifs in the great hall, between the two smoldering log fires. Although he could never be sure who was lurking in the maze of passages, the honeycomb of rooms, which constituted the castle, he judged this to be something like a full turnout.

His host and hostess stood side by side, for all the world like an ordinary husband and wife, while their guests circulated round them. The Countess Betty, still in her riding clothes, in which, Lindsay had to admit, she did not look at all bad, had taken up a position at Philippe's elbow; no matter who spoke to him on what subject, she kept up an intertwined dissertation on horse breeding. Young Christian was carrying on a conversation—apparently amusing—with Prince Cottanero, his lady friend Natasha, and Cousin Odile. The latter caught Lindsay's eye and smiled as soon as he entered the hall, but if this was an invitation for him to try his hand at resistance to hypnosis he ignored it. He joined Françoise, who, with occasional help from her husband—when he could withdraw momentarily from the subject of horses—was entertaining the new arrivals, two of them, and, for Lindsay's money, well up to what he was beginning to regard as the Bellac standard.

He was interested to find that his normal shyness with new acquaintances had altogether vanished, routed by this new-found curiosity—if such a mild word could describe his almost passionate interest in the people around him.

Françoise, her eyes avoiding his, introduced him to the Abbé Luchard and his secretary, Herr Kautzmann. Luchard was a rather fleshily handsome prelate of perhaps fifty; if he looked younger it was because his dark hair had retained—naturally,

Lindsay was inclined to think—its color and thickness. He was a well-upholstered, jovial man—smooth as cream, civilized, never lost for a word, and seldom for a witty one.

His secretary, by way of contrast, was one of those one-colored Germans: hair, face, eyebrows, lips, all a kind of medium beige. His eyes did little to alleviate the boredom because they were so light a blue; they looked as if they had been much washed—but if in tears, than in tears, at the most, of self-pity. His features were absolutely regular, and should have added up to good looks; however, they did not—not even to languid, vapid good looks. He gave the impression that he would remain for the most part silent, like Natasha, but this was unfortunately not the case; he talked a great deal in a humorless but rather lush voice, off which the language of his birth dripped like gobs of cement out of a mixer. He was perhaps twenty-five years old.

It struck Lindsay as odd that a man as obviously cultivated and witty as the abbé should tolerate for one instant this dreary flow of Germanic platitude. But he did, and there must clearly be a reason. Lindsay hoped that the atmosphere of Bellac was not turning him into the kind of bloodless cynic who always jumps at the most obvious and least charitable conclusion.

Herr Kautzmann—his Christian name was Heinz—was holding forth about the castles of the Rhine; he would probably have been hurt if anyone had told him so, but the implication of every word he said was that in Germany there were bigger castles than Bellac, situated in better positions, and infinitely more beautiful. He expressed this opinion obliquely in a tedious recitation of statistics.

The Abbé Luchard, perhaps glad to escape from this performance, which for his own good reasons he would not stem, began to discuss with Lindsay the paintings of Leonardo da Vinci.

During this, Tante Estelle came down the wide staircase deep in conversation with a man whom Lindsay at once guessed to be the village priest. He wore the usual rather ancient soutane, walked with his hands folded in front of him, and was nodding periodically as he listened to the old lady's monologue—for monologue it certainly was.

As they drew nearer, Lindsay heard her say, '... you'll have to advise me; I'm sorry but there it is—I must have been born without the usual moral sense.'

The priest smiled, and it was a delightful smile—warm, friendly, compassionate. He was not a big man, yet he gave an impression of size. He had a brown, wise face and grizzled gray hair cut very short. His eyes were of a startling blue, like two polished pieces of lapis lazuli; they were restless and inquisitive, and, Lindsay thought, if the whole of his personality had not been so kindly they would have been alarming—they were too sharp.

The hand which he offered to Lindsay was dry and hard like a piece of sun-warmed wood. It was impossible not to like him.

He had, Lindsay noticed at once, a curious effect upon the Abbé Luchard. It would not have been surprising if this man—worldly, undoubtedly wealthy, and probably powerful in the hierarchies of the church—had patronized the dusty parish priest a little; on the contrary, the abbé greeted him with something like deference, and the eyes that he turned on his insufferably loquacious secretary were suddenly hard and watchful as he introduced the young man to Père Dominique. There must indeed have been some prior discussion of this unassuming character; Lindsay caught the glance that passed between the abbé and the German, and Herr Kautzmann was suddenly humble—a state, Lindsay thought, almost more revolting than his former arrogance.

It was all very interesting. He tried to catch his hostess's eye to see what she was thinking, but Françoise was still assiduously avoiding him. As before, however, Tante Estelle was doing just the opposite.

'I observe,' she said, 'that you find our guests interesting.'

'You're quite right.'

She nodded, glancing round the hall. 'I have to agree with you; it takes a great deal to drag me away from my little luncheons with the children.' She smiled at his look of surprise.

'But how should you know? Yes, we have the meal together every day; their conversation is better suited to mine—we are all surrealists.'

She was staring at him with the vacant look which he had seen before. It meant, he knew, that she was thinking about a subject far removed from the one she was talking about, and he was not in the least surprised when she performed one of her conversational somersaults and said, 'It has been on my conscience: I was wrong to say the things which I said to you at lunchtime yesterday. It is nothing to do with me whom my nephew asks to stay in his house—now, is it?'

'No. And nothing to do with me either.'

'How wise of you to see that.'

So, he was thinking, Françoise had been right. The old lady was in some way afraid of Philippe.

'You're a very sensible young man,' she was now saying. 'It would be a happier world if everybody realized that nothing is ever gained by meddling in the lives of other people.'

'Live and let live,' said Lindsay vacuously, wondering who else would take time off to offer him oblique warnings.

If indeed there were any truth in what Françoise supposed —if a shadow of death did really hang over her husband—it was alarming how many people seemed to be against any action being taken. A suspicious person could have been forgiven for imagining that these people were actually in favor of Philippe de Montfaucon's departing this life. He decided that it would be interesting to try the direct approach on Tante Estelle. He said, 'Do *you* think that Philippe is afraid of dying?'

She stared at him. 'Of dying! My dear young man, I don't suppose he has given it a thought; in another twenty years maybe ... One does begin to consider such things as middle age draws on.'

He could not tell whether she was genuinely ignorant of the subject under discussion or not; her eyes were at all times too restless ever to betray her in a lie.

'I meant,' he said, 'afraid of dying *soon*. This year, perhaps.'

The effect was not exactly what he had anticipated but it

was disturbing. She shut her mouth tightly and came a step nearer to him; then she gazed into his face in silence for what seemed a long time—he became aware of people glancing at them. At last she said, 'What made you say a thing like that? What have you heard? What has someone been saying to you?'

It was his turn to be oblique. 'I've been reading about the Montfaucon family, and the really extraordinary ends that some of them have met with.'

But, he realized—with something like panic—the old lady was not going to be diverted. She suddenly took hold of his arm with a hand like the talon of a bird; her pale eyes, unblinking, never left his face. 'What did you mean?' she demanded.

Lindsay looked round, appalled. There seemed to be no chance of a movement towards the dining room—and even if there were he very much doubted whether Tante Estelle would release him until he had answered her question. Entirely unable to think of a lie which would seem in the least possible, he fell back on the truth. He said, 'Françoise seems to have some idea . . .'

'Françoise! She said nothing to me.'

He realized three things quite suddenly. First, that the old woman had been expecting this—that it had been at the back of her mind, perhaps for years. Second, that she had not questioned the truth of the idea, only the source from which it had sprung. And third, that now, for the first time, he himself knew—absolutely and without doubt—that unless some action were taken Philippe de Montfaucon was indeed going to die.

Tante Estelle was now seized with an indecision which it was painful to witness. She said, 'It's not possible. Why didn't she . . . ? The child!' She looked towards the stairs, her mouth working, her poise utterly deserting her. Then she looked back at Lindsay, pale eyes wide-open, face alarmingly white. She said again, 'It's not possible. He wasn't even born.' She stared round her as if looking for a way of escape. Then her eyes focused on something or someone just over Lindsay's shoulder. 'No,' she said. And then, very loud, 'No.' Lindsay turned instinctively to see what it was that had produced such a cry; he saw only the wall of the room.

Tante Estelle said, 'The sins of omission, the sins of omission.'

Lindsay, appalled by what he had triggered off, said, 'Please. Let me help you? A little cognac . . . ?'

She evaded the hand he put out to assist her, as if his intention had been murder; then she turned and practically ran across the room to the stairs.

This behavior had naturally provoked a good deal of interest. A dozen pairs of eyes followed her wavering passage up the magnificent staircase; and when she finally vanished from view a dozen pairs of eyes swiveled round to look at Lindsay.

Françoise said, 'Lunch then, everybody—if you're ready.'

She came over to Lindsay, eyes wide. 'James, for heaven's sake . . . !'

'I'm sorry. I mean, it was only a shot in the dark.'

'What did you say to her?'

He looked round at her other guests, who were somewhat unwillingly allowing themselves to be ushered into the dining room. 'What I said's too complicated for now; the important thing is that you're right—Philippe is in danger. What's more, the old girl knows what it is.'

Françoise bit her lip. 'She knows?'

'I think so. She said a lot of very odd things; I hope to God I can remember them.'

Whether it was a conscious and kindly action to assist the functioning of his mental processes Lindsay never knew, but Françoise sat him between herself and the talkative Herr Kautzmann. She was entirely occupied with keeping her guests in order while the young German, discovering that Lindsay was British, embarked on a long, muddled and totally dishonest condemnation of the Nazis, who had apparently been so secretive about their evil deeds that the entire German nation had been hoodwinked into thinking them quite decent fellows; imagine their surprise and horror, et cetera, et cetera.

Lindsay gave himself up entirely to a study of the apocalyptic words of Tante Estelle. Twice she had said, 'It's not possible.' This had meant, 'Dear God, I have always known that this might happen, but I had managed to convince myself that the possibility was remote—to lull myself into a false security. Now, what can I do?'

He nodded to himself over his melon. Yes, it had meant that. In the context, and repeated twice, it could mean nothing else.

Then she had said, 'The child!' And she had looked towards the stairs. She had not said, 'The children!' The implication could only be that she had meant the small boy—they had been speaking of the odd deaths of the Montfaucon males. Therefore the boy, Gilles, was in some way involved in his father's fear of death. How?

Over his trout he remembered that Tante Estelle had also said, 'He wasn't even born.' Who wasn't even born? The boy, Gilles? Or perhaps Philippe himself? What had happened before either one or the other had been born which now had a direct bearing on the possible death of Philippe de Montfaucon?

This multiple problem kept him occupied through a dish of stuffed veal, a coffee mousse, a piece of Camembert and halfway through a peach. At this point he remembered that she had seemed to stare over his shoulder and had said, 'No,' twice (indeed, the second time she had shouted it) and he, turning, had seen only the wall of the great room. Only the wall! But what had been hanging on the wall?

He must have let out some exclamation, for several people looked at him, and Herr Kautzmann, who had been wondering for the hundredth time how the British could be so stupid and survive, was startled out of his train of thought.

Françoise looked rather anxiously at him. The eyes that he turned on her were very bright, almost feverish. 'Listen,' he said. 'You know the wall between the door to the library and the door to the little dining room where we lunched yesterday?'

She nodded.

'Isn't there a picture hanging on it? A portrait?'

'Yes, there is.'

He was sure of this now—sure that the half-demented look she had aimed over his shoulder was directed at a portrait. And she had shouted, 'No. *No.*' His heart pounding, he said, 'Françoise, who is that portrait of?' But he knew the answer even before she gave it.

'Philippe's grandfather. James, what's the matter?'

'Philippe's grandfather,' he said. 'Tante Estelle's father. The one who was so mysteriously killed out hunting.'

Edouard de Montfaucon had been painted in something like his thirty-fifth year. Gazing at the portrait, Lindsay understood the meaning of that rather evasive expression, *in his prime.* Grandfather Edouard, at thirty-five or so, had certainly been in his prime; he was a little like the young Henry the Eighth, but without that ferrety Tudor look, about which Lindsay had never been able to come to a decision: was it indeed a family failing, or merely the result of a fashion in painting?

He stood against a slightly romanticized (the picture was dated 1895) background of the chateau—deer grazed beside the lake; storm clouds were gathering beyond the distant mountains. The man himself was big, bursting with vitality and self-confidence. He was dressed for a day's shooting, a double-barreled sporting gun resting over his arm. The proud head was held well up, and there seemed to be a faintly amused expression about the mouth—recognizably Philippe's mouth—nestling between a luxuriant mustache and a neatly trimmed beard; he seemed to be regarding the man who had painted him with amused impatience. The hair and beard were reddish brown. He looked a formidable character, and it was not easy to imagine him being 'accidentally shot while out hunting.' He did not give an impression of being the kind of man who would allow such a thing to happen. If only Tante Estelle . . .

Lindsay sighed. Where Tante Estelle was concerned *if only* was a forlorn hope. Immediately after luncheon he and

Françoise had gone straight to the wing of the castle in which the old lady had her apartment; they had found the door—and a massive door it was too—bolted against them. Repeated knocking, which Françoise had assured him would be useless, eventually produced a grinding of locks and a crashing of bolts, and, finally, a red, square countenance which belonged to Marianne, Tante Estelle's personal maid. Lindsay had felt that it was only the presence of the marquise which had prevented Marianne from throwing him bodily downstairs—she looked perfectly capable of it.

Her lady, she had said, was suffering from a migraine; had retired to bed with a tisane and a sleeping pill, and was now fast asleep, poor soul. This last with a venomous glance at Lindsay —Marianne had probably elicited from her mistress the immediate cause of her condition.

Françoise assured him that the migraine might well last for a week; she had then left him to his rage of impatience and had herself taken the children to see the dentist in Dennat.

Lindsay grew tired of the sardonic gaze of Edouard de Montfaucon. He turned away across the vast hall, his footsteps echoing up to the vaulted ceiling, and went out into the sunshine.

Where his fellow guests were he had no idea. The chateau had seemed utterly deserted by the time he returned from his vigil outside Tante Estelle's door; he had waited there for another hour after Françoise had gone, in the hope that the old lady might care to see him alone, without her nephew's wife. It was now half past five, and the sun was already low in the sky; he thought that French aristocratic hours of eating seemed to be designed in order to lose the afternoon altogether. Since so many of them spent the afternoon asleep in any case this was probably not a bad idea.

He was strolling down towards the lake, nursing his resentment against Tante Estelle, when his eye was caught by the squat tower of the village church. It struck him suddenly that where there was a church there would be a graveyard, a living (if one could apply that word to it) adjunct of history.

The church was very old—thick and stolid, its massive walls pierced here and there by the most primitive lancet windows. It stood, moreover, on a little knoll, surrounded by glooming yew trees. Clearly it had been built at a time when the river and the lake were less reliable than they were now.

The first thing that caught his eye was that the path to the door was paved in three places with tombstones; to his amazement he saw that this was not a new, if rather sacrilegious way to use old granite, nor was it in any part due to chance. Three ancients—and he was unsurprised to discover that they were all members of the Montfaucon family—had chosen to be laid to rest where the feet of future worshippers would be forever shuffling over them. They had not, however, wanted their identities to be worn away by those feet and had directed, before turning themselves into a pavement, that the details of their mortal struggle should be engraved on an upright headstone beside the path. Two of these headstones had clearly been restored—probably in the nineteenth century—but they were all products of considerable charm and beauty. Alain, Luc and Gregoire de Montfaucon, who had died in 1376, 1530 and 1663 respectively, were the men who had chosen this unusual resting place. Thoughtfully he went into the dim interior of the church.

It was very simple and well used. There was no stained glass; because of the trees that grew so close to it a gentle, subaqueous light played over the rough stone and the plain wood, polished by centuries of use. The altar was the plainest and the most eloquent that he had ever seen, decorated only by a heavy silver crucifix with the figure of Christ hanging from it; a glance told him that it was mediaeval, and absolutely undamaged. There are very few works of man that have survived intact, without later 'improvement,' from those passionate centuries of belief, and they are all tremendous in their impact. The unfumbling certainty of the man who had fashioned this crucifix of Bellac, a man who had been dust for six hundred years, spoke across the centuries with absolute clarity. Lindsay had come to the church to spy; he stood there now, moved to the roots of his being.

He turned sharply and found the priest, Father Dominique, watching him. The priest nodded, as if knowing that the crucifix had done its work. 'You are an artist yourself,' he said.

'Yes. Yes. I . . . I wonder you leave the church open; it must be of incalculable value.'

The priest nodded again, his kind face very placid. 'Indeed, yes; so is the Mona Lisa.'

'I'm sorry, I didn't realize.'

'Ah no, our crucifix is not as well known as she is; but it is too well known for any thief ever to be able to dispose of it.'

'It's curious,' said Lindsay, looking closer. 'The figure of Christ isn't actually nailed to the Cross at all.'

'He rules from the Cross,' said the priest, his blue, quick eyes on the young man's face. 'Is the Cross itself so important?'

Lindsay did not grasp until much later the full strangeness of this remark because his attention had been caught by a forest of candles in the little north transept of the church. He moved towards them, Father Dominique following.

As he expected, the candles were burning before an effigy of the Holy Virgin—a rather dull statuette. But their light revealed something far from dull on the wall to her left; it was a monument, perhaps even a tomb, and the date was 1422. A figure in bas-relief stood, with head raised, under a tree; the figure was that of a man, a soldier, but his sword lay at his feet and both his hands were clasped round what looked like a goblet. Lindsay was not very expert at deciphering Latin inscriptions, and it was a moment before he realized that he was looking at Gils de Montfaucon, poor Gils who had met so unlikely an end when a tree had fallen upon him. And there indeed was the tree, and there was Gils, surprised apparently in drinking a glass of wine.

Lindsay turned to the priest. 'I suppose it *is* a goblet,' he said.

'One imagines so. They are curious, these old tombs.'

'What is the legend? Had he paused for lunch at the time the tree fell on him?'

'It certainly looks like it.'

Lindsay looked more closely at the stylized, yet oddly

immediate carving. It was hard to tell exactly what Gils *was* holding because in the passing of time the stone had become rubbed, defaced. And then he noticed a strange thing: the object in the man's hands was the only part of the carving to be so worn away. Immediately Lindsay thought of the toe of the statue of St. Peter in his great church in Rome—worn by a million kissing lips. He turned, startled, to the priest; the blue uncanny eyes were fixed on him. He remembered how, at their first meeting, he had thought that it was only the kindliness of the man's face that redeemed the eyes from being a little frightening. In the dim, underwater light of his church, timeless on its mound, he was not at all sure how kind that face really was —or rather what exactly was the measure of its kindliness. The question he had been going to ask never reached his lips. As he turned away from the tomb of Gils, he was aware of his heart beating faster than usual.

Father Dominique went with him towards the door; 'escorted him' might have been the better description. At the idea that he was perhaps being seen off the premises, Lindsay's Highland ancestry rose within him. He turned, looking at the priest with interest; the lean, brown face was withdrawn, the remarkable eyes hidden. Lindsay said, 'I was rather hoping to see the tomb of Edouard de Montfaucon—the marquis's grandfather.'

For a moment Father Dominique said nothing; then, 'How curious that you should ask that.'

'Why? Coming of a purely bourgeois family myself, I have to confess that the aristocracy fascinates me—the continuity of it!'

'Curious,' said the priest, 'because somehow I felt you would already know that he is not buried here at all.'

'Really! How should I know?'

'You show such . . . interest in these things.'

Now wait a minute, Lindsay thought. What is this? There seemed to be some sort of publicity about his movements— even about his thoughts.

He was excited suddenly, and when he was excited he was

not always tactful. 'Well,' he said, 'where *is* he buried?'

'Where he died. It was his wish. He was eccentric in many ways—as you have doubtless heard.'

Lindsay had heard no such thing, but he was extremely interested by the gratuitous piece of information. He looked at his watch—half past six.

'Let me see,' he said. 'Where *did* he die? Oh yes, there was some sort of hunting accident, wasn't there? In the forest, I suppose.'

'Precisely. It is some distance away.'

'I've plenty of time.'

'You are indefatigable, monsieur. Let me see then, which is the best way? Round the edge of the lake, I think. You will see a sluice gate; after it the path divides—take the one to the right. There will be men working there; if you are confused, ask them. I warn you—there is nothing to see.'

'It will pass a pleasant hour, Father. Thank you.'

The priest stood in the door of the church, watching him as he walked away.

The one thing which James Lindsay could never afterwards deny was that the whole disastrous incident was entirely his own fault. The only excuse that he could later find was that hounds on the scent have been known, so great their pre-occupation, to run slap-bang into stone walls.

Even when he met the old woman he was too occupied in his own thoughts to evaluate what happened. And what happened was, by any standards, extraordinary enough. What happened was that she spat at him.

Lindsay, who had greeted her politely, was, it is true, a little taken aback; but then the vagaries of very ancient peasant women in foreign lands had always struck him as unusual. This particular old harridan with her dirty sack would probably have thought nothing of relieving herself on the grass verge beside an arterial road, and he therefore saw no reason why she should not, following some devious argument of her own, find his presence objectionable and spit at him to make the fact known. He thought it unfriendly, no more; he was far too interested in the idea that at one time, probably some centuries ago admittedly, the fate of poor Gils de Montfaucon, squashed by a tree, had seemed saintly. He wondered why. The figure on the tomb had been that of a soldier; there had been a cross on his surcoat; the whole thing was probably something to do with the Crusades.

A mile beyond the sluice gate he still had not come to the division of the path of which Father Dominique had spoken. There, however, were the men working whom he had also mentioned: three of them, engaged in clearing the stream that fed the lake: three mahogany-brown figures like wooden carvings of the shepherds from an ancient crib. As he approached them, his mind full of mediaeval imaginings, he thought that if poor Gils himself were to return he would find little changed about the faces or indeed the garb of these men, their trousers tied with string, their shapeless hats on the back of their heads.

'I was looking,' he said, 'for the tomb in the wood—the tomb of the Marquis Edouard.'

The oldest of the three crossed himself. The youngest said to the middle-aged one, 'It's the stranger.'

Now, Lindsay did think this remark rather curious since there were by now so many strangers wandering about Bellac; at that precise moment, however, he was more interested in the old man who had crossed himself.

'Can you tell me the way?'

The middle-aged one said, 'The way is easy.' He made it sound faintly Biblical; later Lindsay was to wonder how intentional this was. He did not intend to be put off by roundabout word play in any case—he had had enough of prevarication, in the person of Tante Estelle, for one day.

'Your priest,' he added, 'told me that I would find a place where the path divided.'

The young man said, 'Père Dominique.'

Lindsay was getting impatient.

'He was buried,' the old man announced, 'on the very spot where he fell. But they carried him first.'

Lindsay stared at the weatherbeaten, lined face; two brilliant blue eyes looked out of it, as if periwinkles had flowered out of a gnarled tree stump.

'Carried him?'

'To the castle,' said the young man impatiently.

Lindsay, wondering whether there might not be a well of folklore to be tapped here, said, 'It was a hunting accident, wasn't it?'

The old man said, 'I remember it—only ten years old, I was. Seven carried him, and seven came after.'

The middle-aged man pointed up the path. 'You'll find the turning just in the trees there.'

'Thank you.'

'If it isn't a rude question, what might your interest be?'

'Just curiosity. It seems strange that he wasn't buried in the churchyard.'

The three faces were blank, staring at him. Eventually the youngest said, 'A man can lie where he likes.'

The old man said, 'Ay, and he rests there. No more was heard of him. There's some buried in hallowed ground don't lie so easy.'

At this the three of them exchanged a look. Then, as if by mutual consent, they returned to their work.

Lindsay, dismissed, continued on his way; yet, as he reached the trees and came to the division of the path, something made him look back. The three men were leaning on their implements staring after him, as motionless as the tree trunks they so closely resembled. They were the last human beings he saw on his journey to the tomb of Grandfather Edouard. They were, almost, the last human beings he saw in his life.

9

The Unknown Hunters

Lindsay could not agree with Father Dominique that Edouard de Montfaucon's last resting place was uninteresting. By the time he reached it the sun had gone down behind the mountains, yet the sky overhead was still golden; the forest seemed to have been beaten out of bronze—dark, metallic.

For some time the path had twisted and turned, climbing steeply between dank rocks, lichen stained. On this sunless side of the bluff that overhung the lake, ivy and elder and yew created a Gothic gloom. Through the tree trunks and far below, smooth water reflected the golden sky. Presently the path had leveled out; elder and yew gave way to oak and beech, and there, at the edge of a rough clearing, was the tomb.

It was absolutely plain: a big slab of black marble raised a foot above the ground. The extraordinary thing about it was that it might have been put there that very morning instead of some sixty years before; whereas the rocks near to it were overgrown with moss and lichen and ivy, Grandfather Edouard's gravestone hardly carried a speck of dust. The inscription chiseled upon it stood out boldly—boldly and mysteriously. In the first place there were no dates, merely the name, EDOUARD DE MONTFAUCON. Above this was inscribed, 'I would be saved and I would save, Amen.' And below it, 'The Twelve dance on high, Amen. The Whole on high hath part in our dancing. Amen. Whoso danceth not, knoweth not what cometh to pass. Amen.'

Lindsay stood there for some time, frowning over these words, while the gold faded from the sky over his head, and the bronze-green shadows of the forest darkened towards night.

He felt sure that the words were part of the Bible; the *Twelve* must surely be the Apostles, and that indicated the

New Testament; yet the New Testament, as far as he could remember in his ignorance, had never spoken of dancing.

He was musing along these lines when something caught his attention. He could never decide later whether he had seen a movement or heard a sound that was not in the pattern of the place—or whether, indeed, there was inside him some buried forest sense that warned him of danger.

He turned his head sharply, peering into the shadows; he was slightly taken aback to find how swiftly darkness was falling. As far as he could tell nothing moved. His nerves were tingling now. Beyond the clearing the path plunged over the edge of the bluff in a black thicket of yew trees; it looked uninviting, to put it mildly, and yet it was the only way back to the chateau that he knew.

But what had he seen or sensed? A little breeze stirred in the leaves above him. Somewhere down in the valley a cockerel was crowing, and the sound was oddly reassuring. He took one pace towards the path, and then stopped dead, his scalp prickling; for something *had* moved this time—there was no doubt about it. Yes, there was someone standing behind that leaning beech tree. The edge of a shoulder blurred the smooth line of the trunk—or was it a knot in the wood, the stump of a broken branch?

He stood there undecided, half mocking himself for this display of nerves, half sure that his senses had not betrayed him. The shadows deepened a little. And still he stood, not liking the idea of that steep path among the yews, damp and slippery underfoot.

Then, quite softly and seeming very close, a man's voice began to sing. Lindsay took a step back and felt the hard edge of the black-marble tombstone against his calf. There was something very frightening indeed about this quiet song coming out of the gathering darkness—frightening, and mocking. Ridiculously enough, what struck him at that moment as being most sinister about the song was the fact that he could not understand the words; they were either in the local patois or in Old French. It was like being insulted in a language one does not know and cannot reply to. Then, to his left, the shadows stirred; he glimpsed a man moving, and not quickly, from one tree trunk to the next. Out of the corner of his eye he caught another movement far away to his extreme right. He turned sharply, just in time to see another man. The singing stopped abruptly, and there was absolute silence. Again a small breeze wandered through the leaves and left them chattering.

He did not so much see the lump of rock coming as sense it. He ducked, and it hit his shoulder, knocking him halfway across the gravestone; as he recovered himself he saw that the clearing was alive with moving shadows. He jumped over the stone and began to run. At the same moment a dog behind him let out a deep bark that tailed away into excited howling. Lindsay's blood froze. The impossible fact was true (eruptions of physical violence into everyday life always struck him as faintly impossible): he was being hunted—hunted across country that was absolutely strange to him, by men who very probably knew every inch of it.

The point was that ahead of him lay the whole expanse of the bluff. What was it they called it? La Bosse. He very much doubted that he had the physical energy to cross it at the double with brambles and bracken tearing at his legs and low-hanging branches slashing him over the face at every other step.

He paused for a moment. The crashing in the undergrowth behind told him all that he needed to know; there was no other sound, no shouting of voices to give a human quality to the chase.

He reasoned that if they intended to kill him they would urge him towards the lake—towards the black cliffs, too steep for any but the hardiest tree to cling to, which fell sheer to the water. He veered away to his right, keeping to flat ground.

His breath was already beginning to come in gasps. Twice he fell, the second time across a hidden jagged rock that made him cry out in pain. He realized that the ground was still sloping upwards: he had not yet reached the top of the bluff, let alone begun the descent on the other side of it. The chilling knowledge was borne upon him that he would not be able to do it—in open country there might have been a hope, but among the traps and pitfalls of the undergrowth failure was certain. Well then, what alternative?

There was, he knew, only one. It might just conceivably work if chance would present him with the right terrain to carry it out: he would suddenly stop running, dive under cover, try to control the gasping for breath that seemed to be tearing him in half, and hope that they might pass him by—hope that the dog, if there was only *one* dog, would not be immediately behind him and right on his track.

He paused again. Yes, they were much nearer. He stood there, panting, staring wildly round him into the gathering darkness.

It took him a moment to realize that chance was indeed offering him what he sought, but that it was not on the ground where he was looking for it. An oak tree, not four yards away, divided, some three feet above his head, into two great branches. He ran forward and jumped, clawing at the rough bark, tearing his fingernails, searching desperately for a hold. Somehow or other his hand encountered a small branch. One enormous heave and a wild scrabbling of feet and he lay on his stomach looped over the fork of the tree. He pulled up his legs quickly and crouched there, clinging, his face pressed against the bark, his heart pounding.

A moment later the bushes below him were thrust aside and the dark figure of a man lurched past, followed by another who was being dragged by a large, a very large, black dog on a leash. To right and left of him Lindsay could hear other bodies crashing through the undergrowth. He would dearly have liked to stay where he was, clutching the friendly oak; but he knew that this was the one impossible thing. The dog had evidently been carried past the end of his scent by its own impetus and excitement, but it would return. A shout told him that already it had faltered; he could hear it whining.

He dropped out of the tree and doubled back the way he had come. For the first time, so topsy-turvy is the working of the brain under stress, he found himself wondering exactly *who* these men were; perhaps the fact that he had now actually seen two of them made the whole matter more personal . . .

But all thought was banished by a sudden deep baying from the dog behind him; it meant, he thought, only one thing: they had unleashed it. At the idea of this, panic seized him. He no longer made any effort to conserve his energy, to think, to use the brain which, alone, gave him an advantage. Stumbling, falling, gasping for breath—a mindless, terrified animal himself—he floundered through the thick, damnable undergrowth, hearing only the sound of the dog, or possibly dogs, behind him.

Suddenly, to his horror, the ground began to fall away under his feet; he caught the glimmer of water far below. He realized that fear had caused him to lose all sense of direction. He turned sharply to his left, slipping and scrabbling up the slope. Out of the corner of his eye he caught a glimpse of the dog —it was some kind of Alsatian—and at the same moment he reached level ground again. He found himself running down a path he had never seen before, a broad ride through the trees, but he knew that the dog was gaining on him; moreover, there was a commotion some twenty yards ahead, and two men ran out into the ride, coming towards him. He realized that he was trapped, and the realization made him pause for a fraction of a second. In that fraction of a second the dog sprang. Mercifully he managed to dodge. The hurtling body, teeth snapping, hit only his shoulder; he caught the rank smell of its breath. He spun round and found himself looking at a man, arm raised to strike him. The club, or whatever it was, crashed down onto the side of his neck, and he fell, crying out at the pain.

What happened next was very confused. He was aware of a shot ringing out, and then of a close-up view of a heavy boot in the moment before it kicked him hard on the forehead. The blow must have almost knocked him out, yet he had time to think, God, I hope they shoot me, at least it's quick —time also to grab the kicking leg and wrap his arms round it. Its owner went down with a satisfactory thud, swearing. Lindsay thought, Where's the dog? A second shot rang out, yet he was still alive. Then he heard the drumming of horses' hooves, glimpsed the animal right over him. He rolled away from the leg which he was still grasping and came face to face with the Alsatian, but it was lying on its side and it was dead. An instant later a man's body seemed to drop out of the sky; he held a heavy crop of some kind, and he was raising it to strike. Lindsay covered his head with his arms and shut his eyes. But no blow fell—or rather, as he found when he opened his eyes again, not in his direction; one of his attackers was receiving the full force of the crop in his face—he fell back with a howl of pain and went down on his knees.

There was a sudden silence. In the twilight Lindsay could see half-a-dozen men standing quite still, their heads hanging sheepishly. The horseman turned and knelt swiftly, and Lindsay found himself looking into the eyes of Philippe de Montfaucon. Then—either from pure relief or merely as a result of the blow on the head—he passed out.

After this there were glimmerings of consciousness, but they were no more than shadows on a screen: he was being carried; he was being washed; a face that he knew swam forward out of darkness, and then there was a sharp, agonizing pain in the side of his head and darkness returned—a vortex of darkness dragging him down into unconsciousness. The next thing was a voice speaking very clearly: '. . . extremely thick skull—really most remarkable . . . Rest, of course . . . Complications most unlikely . . . Skull . . .' And at some point he saw the bright needle of a hypodermic syringe lying on the flesh of his arm.

Then the darkness began to weave in front of his eyes, making odd patterns. He found that he felt pleasantly drowsy, but not in any way sick. The patterns collected themselves into recognizable shapes, and suddenly he was awake, blinking.

He was in a room that he had never seen before, lying on a very comfortable sofa with a rug over him. From the shape of the room (it was almost circular) he guessed that this was the ancient tower, the keep, which Grandfather Edouard had converted into a self-contained apartment. The door which he could see was undoubtedly the door through which—and it seemed years ago—he had watched Odile de Caray disappearing with the dead body of the white dove. Somehow he had imagined splendors of luxury behind that door, but, in fact, the room was austere. What furniture there was seemed to be of plain wood, beautiful and black with age; since the walls themselves were white, the only color came from a crimson carpet which completely covered the floor.

Not far from the sofa, in a pool of warm light, Philippe de Montfaucon was playing chess with the Abbé Luchard, their two intelligent faces gravely inclined over the board. The boy, Christian, sat cross-legged on the floor with a guitar; he could hardly have been said to be playing it, but he was striking successions of chords, major melting into minor, discord resolving into harmony. Lindsay found this rather astonishing; he had never supposed that the young man would have a note of music in him—and yet this endless series of improvised chords was wonderfully soothing. He closed his eyes and presumably slept again, for when he next opened them, Philippe was standing beside the sofa, looking down on him. The Abbé Luchard still sat at the chess table, staring at the pieces. Christian lay on the floor asleep, the guitar on his chest.

Lindsay struggled to sit up; his head was aching abominably, and he could only suppose that the effect of whatever had been in the hypodermic had worn off.

Philippe de Montfaucon said, 'Lie still. The doctor has been to see you. He says that there is no concussion; he went away full of admiration for the quality of your skull. Now it's time that the wound was dressed.'

The Abbé Luchard had risen from the chess table. 'My dear young man,' he said, 'when you ride with Philippe you must do as I do—always ask for the oldest mount in his stable. Good horsemen have no idea how difficult it is to sit on a horse.'

Lindsay, watching Philippe's eyes, which were regarding him sternly, merely nodded. After he had thought about the situation for a moment he said, 'Oh, it wasn't the horse's fault; he must have stumbled over a rock.'

Philippe said, 'I think so. It's a good thing I was with you. Now, about that bruise . . .'

He went to the fireplace and tugged at a bell pull which hung beside it. Looking down at the sleeping boy, he said, 'Don't be alarmed by Mère Blossac. Her looks are against her and she doesn't wash as much as she might, but on the other hand dear old Dr. Chauvet never cured a cut or a bruise as quickly as she does.'

At that moment the door opened and an old woman came shuffling in; she was so busy bowing to the marquis that she did not at once see her patient lying on the sofa. Lindsay thus had time to get used to the idea that his nurse was to be the harpy who had spat at him on the road, whereas she, on turning, was taken entirely by surprise.

She glared at him, turned back to Philippe de Montfaucon, and said, '*Him?*'

Her seigneur nodded gravely. She looked again at Lindsay and shrugged as if to say, Well, some people have the oddest friends. Then she came forward and bent over him.

It was perfectly true that she had a powerful and unusual smell to her, but it was not actively unpleasant, reminding him more of animals and hay and maquis than anything else. In any case he was too astonished by her hands to worry about smells; they were incredibly light, gentle, deft for one so old. She worked with the absolute concentration of the expert; she whipped off the dressing that the doctor had put on Lindsay's forehead and examined the wound minutely, hissing through her teeth. Where the cosh had landed on the side of his neck there was only a bruise, but the old woman was clearly not impressed by the way the doctor had treated it; she shook her head wisely over the idiocies of science.

Then, out of her sack, she produced a small spirit lamp. She lit it carefully and placed over it a tin of what looked like black treacle. Presently this mixture began to give off a most alarming smell. While it was heating she produced from the sack a bundle of dried leaves—large, serrated leaves from a tree which Lindsay could not place—and when the potent-smelling treacle was at exactly the right temperature she spread some of it on the leaves, clapped it over the wound and bound it in place with the doctor's bandage—or rather half the doctor's bandage. The other half she rolled up and popped into the sack for future use, doubtless on a more deserving patient.

As for the bruise, she uncorked a large preserving jar in which was a mash of leaves and herbs; she put two spoonfuls of it onto the doctor's piece of cotton wool and strapped it in place with the remains of his adhesive tape. Privately Lindsay thought her treatment of the bruise slightly cavalier—until he discovered, next day, that all the pain had gone out of it. Finally, after feeling his pulse with the tip of one dry old finger, she poured into a wineglass, which Philippe produced for her, a measure of some greenish mixture smelling rather like rotten senna pods. This she held out to Lindsay. He looked nervously at it.

Philippe said, 'It's only a sedative; I've had it myself dozens of times.'

The old woman grinned at the face which he pulled after drinking the stuff; then, her work done, she turned to Philippe, bobbed a sort of curtsey, crossed herself, and scurried out of the room.

Philippe and the Abbé Luchard were obviously amused by the expression on Lindsay's face.

'Oh yes,' said the abbé, 'she's a witch, all right. Never underestimate the knowledge of a witch; mankind has forgotten more things, and more important things, than he will ever learn.' He glanced at his watch. 'Three o'clock. High time I was in bed.' He bowed to Philippe and then to Lindsay and turned to the door. Christian still slept on the floor, holding his guitar.

Luchard paused for a moment looking down at the sleeping youth. 'I often wonder,' he said, 'what is innocence? Good night. God be with you.'

Philippe de Montfaucon turned and looked at Lindsay, a wary, thoughtful look; then he went over to the young man, knelt beside him and passed his fingers lightly over the guitar. Christian woke up at once, without fuss; he sat up, yawning.

Philippe said, 'Go to bed. It's three o'clock.'

The boy nodded, stood up, slung the guitar over his shoulder and yawned again, stretching like a young animal. 'Couldn't we go out?' he said. 'Couldn't we ride up to the waterfall?'

Philippe shook his head, smiling. Christian looked across at Lindsay, shrugged and walked out of the room.

The two men stared at each other for a time in silence. At length Lindsay said, 'Obviously it wasn't just *chance* that you were there.'

'Why "obviously"?'

'It was hardly the time of day the Lord of the Manor would choose to ride around his estates.'

Philippe de Montfaucon looked at him, smiling. 'My dear James, I don't think you realize how big this place is—there are parts of it that I must leave at midday if I want to get back to the chateau by nightfall.'

'I still don't think it was chance,' said Lindsay obstinately.

The other man sat down at the chess table and began to make patterns with the pieces. 'Tell me what you *do* think then, James.'

'I think—God knows how—that you ... you knew what those men meant to do. I think you followed them.'

Philippe nodded. There was a kind of sadness about his face that Lindsay found touching; he remembered suddenly that he owed his life to this man, whatever the circumstances. He said, 'I haven't thanked you. Another couple of minutes ...'

He remembered the rank smell of the dog's breath, the whiteness of those teeth that might have found a hold on his throat.

'For God's sake,' he said, 'what have they got against me?'

Philippe de Montfaucon picked up a white knight and examined it carefully. 'I imagine,' he said, 'that they think you are being too inquisitive about things which ... which they hold to be private and perhaps sacred.'

The mixture that Mère Blossac had seen fit to put onto the wound felt as if it were slowly eating its way into his forehead. He would dearly have liked to rip off the dressing, yet, almost in spite of himself, he had an absolute trust in her methods; it was as if the sureness of those old fingers had stirred in him an ancient, long-lost belief. However he could no longer sit still. He pushed the blanket off his legs and swung them off the sofa; it was a far from easy matter getting to his feet, but after the initial dizziness, when he thought that he must surely fall flat on his face, he managed to perch on the arm. In this position he felt less helpless.

Philippe, he noticed, respected his wish for independence; he did not scurry forward to help him as a woman would have done. But the look which he gave him said very clearly, You are on the brink of a discussion in which I don't propose to take part.

Lindsay said, 'I wasn't aware that I was being inquisitive about anything that remotely affected your peasants.'

With a gentleness which could not hide the irony, the Frenchman replied, 'But then you are aware of very little here, James; I think we should consider that fact.'

Lindsay knew that he must feel his way carefully towards the center of this conversation, which would have been difficult enough if he had been in complete control of his faculties. He decided to approach from another angle.

'I can't deny that the whole thing was my fault; it isn't as though I hadn't been warned to keep my nose out of . . . out of your affairs.'

'Warned!' There was no doubt about the surprise in the other man's voice.

Lindsay told him about the Montfaucon history which had been so mysteriously transformed into a book of fairy tales. Philippe smiled. 'I have . . . young friends who sometimes take me at my word a little too quickly. For a guest in my house, you *have* taken rather a lot upon yourself.'

Lindsay said, 'Don't you think my reasons for doing so excuse me to a certain extent?'

The handsome face clouded for a moment. 'How should I know your reasons?' he said.

Lindsay leaned forward. 'Would it surprise you to know

that you are the best friends I ever had, you and Françoise?'

'Long ago, James. Long ago.'

'Does time have anything to do with it, Philippe? Do you think I didn't suffer with you when you showed me your vines yesterday?'

Suddenly the withdrawn, almost disinterested expression of the other man's face infuriated him. He burst out. 'All right. Maybe I am being curious—and I know it's none of my business—but what about Françoise?'

'Ah, Françoise ...' Philippe de Montfaucon put the white knight back onto the chessboard and stood up. He came across the room to where Lindsay still leaned, a trifle unsteadily, against the arm of the sofa, and stood looking at him.

Lindsay, whose vision—what with sedatives and blows on the head—was none too clear that night, was amazed to see that Philippe had changed physically since their last meeting. He had thought then that the years had refined this face, giving to it an austerity, almost a beauty, which it had never possessed before; and now, only a few days later, he saw that this process was continuing: the skin was stretched a little too tightly over the fine bones, and the dark eyes seemed more brilliant, yet in some way set deeper under the sharply defined, black brows. He wondered again whether perhaps the answer to the whole problem was not indeed that most simple one—that this man was dying slowly of some wasting disease, and would not disclose the fact to his wife. And yet, at the same moment that he thought this, he knew that there was nothing simple about Philippe de Montfaucon, or about Bellac.

'Yes, Françoise ...' He said it again, softly, not taking those deep-set eyes off the man in front of him. 'You love her, don't you, James? You always have.'

'So did you—once.'

'Yes. Once.' And suddenly a terrible thing happened. That noble face, so fine-drawn, so austere, began to crumple before Lindsay's appalled eyes; it was as if an invisible hand was pulling the bones away from inside it.

Philippe de Montfaucon said, 'Oh God, dear God ... Show

me, show me ...' And he turned away, pressing his hands over his face. He went to the window and stood, his forehead against the glass, while his body was racked with a succession of great shudders that seemed to come up out of the center of his being; but he made no sound.

And Lindsay—his head threatening to split open, and his literally battered brain reeling in its effort to grasp what was happening—remembered what Françoise had said sitting under that willow tree beside the lake. With a passion of certainty she had said it: 'I believe he needs help desperately; he needs friends ... I *know* the moment will come when he'll turn away from whatever it is that possesses him. At that moment —at that one moment—he will need help.'

And this, Lindsay was horrified to realize, was that one moment. Françoise was not here, and he himself was not going to be able to grasp it; his limp, drugged brain and this agonizing pain in his forehead were going to defeat him. Yet somehow he must try, he *must* reach this man's heart and touch it, for the chance would certainly never return.

He managed a few steps towards the window, and said, 'Philippe, what is it? For God's sake let me help you.'

There was no answer. Philippe rolled his head from side to side against the windowpane; he was still shuddering.

Lindsay said, 'Whatever it is, it's here at Bellac. Don't you see that you must break with it? Get away, Philippe; get right away from Bellac—you could take Christian with you, if that's what you want, and put a thousand miles between you and this place.'

In the dead husk of a voice Philippe de Montfaucon said, 'I once ... once put half the world between myself and Bellac.' He gripped the frame of the window in an effort to still that terrible shuddering. 'And when I came at last, they ... they said they were expecting me.'

He turned suddenly then, and his eyes were quite wild, the eyes of a hunted man. 'But I *could* go. Would you help me, James? Would you come with me and stay with me?'

'You know I would.' For a moment he really did think that

he had triumphed over his own limitations—he really did think that in some way he had reached out a hand across the vast distances of the soul that separated him from this man. Then, to his bitter disappointment, he saw that fanatic light die out of the dark eyes. Philippe turned back to the window, shaking his head. 'No,' he said. 'No, no, no. What am I talking about?'

Lindsay said, 'Do it. Please do it. You could if you wanted to.'

'I could—*if* I wanted to.'

Lindsay knew then that the moment had passed, and that he had failed.

Philippe said, 'I have work to do here.' It was a good imitation of his ordinary everyday voice. He turned from the window and went across to the fireplace, where there was a tray of drinks; he poured himself a brandy, looked up at Lindsay and said, 'No, not for you. Doctor's orders.'

Lindsay shook his head. 'Damn the doctor. Mère Blossac wouldn't mind.'

Philippe poured brandy into two glasses and gave him one.

'Please,' Lindsay said. 'Don't shut yourself off from ...'

The other overrode him, his voice steely. 'I'm very tired; I don't know what happened to me just now.'

'You were afraid,' said Lindsay, taking his courage in both hands. 'Afraid of dying.'

There was a sudden stillness in the room. Philippe de Montfaucon's face hardened; fine-drawn in any case, it became now a face of stone.

'We must all die,' he said softly.

'Afraid of dying,' Lindsay said, 'before September.'

After a moment the other nodded. 'Françoise again?'

'Yes. Good God, can't you understand what all this is doing to her?'

'I thought that perhaps ... I had stopped her loving me.'

'You have—in one sense.'

Philippe nodded. 'She asked you down here, I know that. I suppose you met in Paris.'

'We did—by chance.'

'You can call it chance if you like; I would give it a bigger name. No matter.' His voice now sounded unutterably weary; it was clear that he had passed through some kind of ordeal —the ordeal by temptation perhaps. He passed a hand over his eyes. 'James, I was going to ask . . . no, demand that you go back to Paris first thing in the morning. No, don't interrupt. What I have to say now is very difficult, but I see that it must be said. Sit down—you look ghastly.'

Lindsay obeyed. Whatever it was that Mère Blossac had put on his wound, it was now doing its work. The pain had gone and a kind of warm, enveloping glow had taken its place.

Philippe said, 'A few hours ago you came within inches—or seconds, if you like—of meeting a very unpleasant end. I can't guarantee that it won't happen again.'

'Oh yes, you can. Those men will do anything for you.'

'Exactly. That's the whole point. They will kill you—for me. Don't ask questions because I shall not answer, but that is what they thought they were doing.'

Lindsay could barely grasp the sense of this, but, dimly, he could see that there was sense there.

'I was going to make you leave Bellac, James, because I don't want you to be killed. I realize now that if you stop prying into . . . into what does not concern you, you will be safe; but *only* if you stop prying. Is that clear?'

'Perfectly.'

'Will you promise me that you'll stop?'

'No.'

Philippe shook his head, eyeing his friend with a sort of humorous exasperation. 'I think perhaps you *will* stop, though —if not for me, then for Françoise. Because you do love her, don't you?'

'You know I do.'

The husband of Françoise put his fingertips to his forehead for a moment as if trying to still the thoughts that rioted there; then he said, 'Would you still marry her—if she were free?'

'She isn't free.'

'Would you, James?'

'Yes.'

Philippe nodded—and then, after a moment, he sighed; it was a deep, deep sigh. 'No,' he said. 'It was not chance that you met in Paris. I want you to stay here; and I want you to know —because this *is* important, James—that I ... that it would make me very happy if I could think that you were going to marry her.'

He saw Lindsay's protest rising to the surface and waved it aside. 'All right, then, since you force me to say it—not that it will make any difference—I want you to marry her *when I am dead.*'

Somehow Lindsay managed to get to his feet again—found enough breath to actually shout, 'For God's sake ...'

But by that time Philippe de Montfaucon was at the door. 'For God's sake, if you like,' he said. 'I'll send my man to take you to your room. Good night, James.'

'But I can help you,' Lindsay cried. 'Don't you see that? I can save you.'

Philippe shook his head. 'You can't. Believe me, my dear old friend, you can't. You don't know, you see; you don't know what *is,* so how can you know what will be?'

Lindsay never knew what it was in these words that sparked off that quirk of memory; perhaps, indeed, there was an instinctive knowledge in him deeper than the knowledge of mere intelligence. He suddenly saw in his mind's eye the black slab of marble, solitary in a clearing in a forest—and he remembered what was written on it. He said, '"Whoso danceth not, knoweth not what cometh to pass." Is that it?'

Philippe de Montfaucon was very still, motionless in the doorway; it was as if the phrase had transfixed him there forever. Then at last, without another word, he crossed himself, and was gone.

'Oh God,' said Lindsay aloud to the empty room. 'That *is* it.'

10

The Thirteen Days

He knew that he had the answer; the answer was round and light like a bubble of glass, like a superfine goldfish bowl, and he was running through a forest of almost impenetrable undergrowth pursued by a pack of baying wolves, and he was carrying this delicate bubble of an answer, terrified that he would fall and drop it. Now the wolves were snapping at his heels; he tripped and fell, and the answer slipped from his fingers and went bouncing down the hillside towards the lake; and Philippe de Montfaucon was bending over him, slapping his face and saying, 'You are not to sleep any more. Wake up now. You are not to sleep any more . . .'

Then he was propped up in bed, in his own room at Bellac, and a red-faced man with a stethoscope hanging round his neck was slapping his face and swearing at him.

'You are not to sleep any more. Can you hear me? Wake up at once. Come on, wake up . . .'

Beyond him stood Françoise, biting the back of her fore-finger, a look of distaste on her beautiful face.

Lindsay said, 'All right, all right, I'm awake.'

'Then stay awake,' said the doctor, shaking him by the shoulders.

Lindsay became aware of the fact that the room was filled with sunshine, and something about this struck him as vaguely unsatisfactory. At the same time he began to wonder what had happened to the glass bauble he had been carrying; he couldn't remember seeing it actually hit the lake—so that now, the wolves having vanished for the time being, it might be a good idea to go and see if he could find it . . .

Again the stethoscope began to wave about in front of his eyes, and again he woke up to find that his face was being rudely slapped. He said, 'Do you mind? I've hurt my head, and you aren't doing it any good.'

Then Françoise was making him drink coffee, very strong black coffee. After four cups he began to feel better. The doctor was standing at the window in the sunshine. Ah yes, the sunshine; it never came into this room except during the afternoon. The *afternoon*! And the last thing he could remember was being escorted from Philippe's private sanctum by a muscular manservant; that had been in the middle of the night.

He said, 'What's the time?'

Françoise stroked his hair back from his forehead. 'Five o'clock; don't worry about it.'

At this the doctor turned from the window. 'Worry about it to this extent, young man: don't go swilling down any more of that Blossac woman's potions.'

Françoise said, 'There was nothing he could do about it; I tell you he was unconscious.' And to Lindsay, by way of explanation, she added. 'I caught one of the servants giving you the stuff; you were still asleep.'

'You mean they . . .'

But Françoise, who had her back to the doctor, made an exceedingly savage grimace to him, and he shut his mouth quickly.

The doctor said, 'Your husband's just like the rest of them; they've always had this trust in their wise old women.' He came forward and tilted Lindsay's head backwards so that he could look at his forehead. 'I must say that in certain cases the hag gets some incredible results; if anyone had told me last night . . .' He shook his head.

Lindsay was, now that he came to think of it, aware that there was hardly any pain in the wound at all. As for the bruise on his shoulder, it felt no more than stiff.

The doctor said, 'Now—are you going to stay awake? I'm late for my surgery as it is.'

Françoise stood up. 'I can manage.'

'You'll have to watch him. If he takes any more of that stuff . . .'

'I won't,' said Lindsay, 'now that I know what they . . . Now that I know you don't want me to.'

While Françoise was seeing the doctor out, he decided that he had been in bed long enough. Accordingly he threw back the bedclothes and swung his feet to the floor. A second later the crash of his falling brought her running back into the room. He was lying on his face, quite unable to get up.

Françoise helped him onto his hands and knees, and, with her assistance, he managed to crawl between the sheets again. Lying back, exhausted by all this, he suddenly became aware of the fact that she was crying; she sat in the chair beside the bed staring at him while the tears rolled down her cheeks. He was appalled. He cried out, 'Françoise . . . !'

'I . . . was so . . . afraid,' she said. 'Why don't you . . . *tell* me what you're going to do?'

A moment later she was on her knees by the bed and he had his arms round her; he was surprised to find that he felt rather like crying himself.

Between sniffs she was saying, '. . . some silly story about falling off a horse . . . and then he said Dr. Chauvet was looking after you, and . . . and I came to see you, and there you were, looking as if you were dead. And Philippe said the doctor had . . . had given you a sedative and you weren't to be disturbed. How *dared* he?' She looked up, anger vanquishing tears. 'It was only by chance I came back to see how you were, and caught that wretched Pierre slopping this stuff down you. Thank goodness, I kept my head. I didn't let him see that I knew what he was doing. As soon as he'd gone I sent for the doctor.'

Lindsay pulled her down against him and kissed her hair, soothing her like a child. Reason shone through the clouds that Mother Blossac's potions had blown into his head; he understood that Françoise loved him, and this was so overwhelming that the next realization took a little while to break through. When it did, however, he found it profoundly unsettling: he understood that it was imperative for this love that Philippe de Montfaucon should live; when this shadow had passed from all their lives, he would ask her to marry him, and she would accept—he was quite sure of this now. But if Philippe were to die, the shadow of that death would fall between them and force them apart; if Philippe were to die they would come to feel that it had been their fault—that, subconsciously, they had not done all that they might have done to prevent it.

At the knowledge of this he was filled with a kind of panic. Two things suddenly emerged from the nightmare of the previous night: one was the memory of Philippe saying, with absolute assurance, absolute acceptance, the words 'when I am dead'; the other was the fact that for a moment, an electrifying moment, he had turned towards the idea of escape—he had admitted that his private nemesis, whatever it was, *could* be avoided.

Françoise said, 'Tell me then. Tell me what really happened.'

He told her; but he did not, he could not, tell her everything. How was it possible to say to a woman, 'Your husband said that he would like me to marry you'? He also left out those words of doom—'When I am dead.' He was too afraid of what they might mean to her and to him. He was already consumed with a desire to be on his feet again, to attack Philippe again, forcing him to see that there was, that there must be a way out.

When he had finished speaking they stared at each other blankly, searching their minds for an answer to the questions that crowded in on them.

Lindsay said, 'But *why* did those men attack me? Admittedly I've been rather nosy about Philippe's affairs, not to mention his ancestors, but why should *they* want me dead? If Philippe had put them up to it ...'

'No,' she cried.

'Well, of course no; he stopped them, didn't he? He saved me from them; but if he had, I could understand it, there might be some kind of logic behind it. Oh no, they acted on their own—and yet, last night, he said, "They were trying to kill you *for* me."' He shook his head bemusedly. 'You don't think ... ? I mean he struck me as being a rather remarkable man, a good man, but you don't think the priest ...'

'Father Dominique!' She was horrified.

'I'm sorry. But he definitely didn't want me to visit Grand-father Edouard's grave.'

Françoise said, 'He *is* a good man; he's one of the few people here I've always been able to turn to. James, I *confess* to him.'

Lindsay nodded. No Catholic himself, he remained unimpressed by the Confessional. 'All right,' he said. 'Why, then, was he so unwilling for me to see that grave in the forest? Because of what was written on it?'

'Hardly.'

'But, Françoise, what other reason could there be?'

Thoughtfully she said, 'He's been upset, I know, by ... by people like Mère Blossac. I can't see why and I told him so. You always get that sort of thing in real country places—harmless, and useful kinds of witchcraft. Such a stupid name for it!'

Lindsay nodded. 'I thought about that. The doctor said that Philippe's people had always relied on it; and I *did* see that girl, Odile, going into the tower with the dead bird. And there's no doubt that he's ... almost worshipped here by some of the peasants ...'

'I wondered if you'd notice that.'

'You can't miss it. But witchcraft isn't the answer; that isn't what drives Philippe. A man who spends hours—as much as twelve hours, didn't you say?—on his knees in front of the altar isn't a pagan; just the opposite—he's almost too much of a Christian.'

Again they were both silent.

Lindsay groaned, pressing his cheek into the pillow. 'What drives me mad is that I *know* the answer; it's here, in my head, and I can't see it. I must know—or why this desire to keep me out of the way, drugged?' He stared at her, arrested by a thought. 'And anyway, Françoise, what's behind this drugging business? It couldn't be kept up forever, could it? Doesn't it mean that there's something happening now, or something just about to happen, which they're afraid I'll understand? Françoise, it must mean that.' He was excited now; he sat bolt upright in bed, and the sudden movement caused his head, apparently, to float upward from his body; he lost his balance again, and flopped back onto the pillow. 'Goddam the old bitch. What the hell's *in* that muck of hers anyway?'

'Poppy heads, boiled, among other things—according to Dr. Chauvet.' She broke off, staring at him. 'Les Treize Jours,' she said. 'Tomorrow.'

Lindsay barely stopped himself sitting up abruptly again.

'It must be that.' She seized his hand and gripped it tightly.

'Describe it to me. What happens? Françoise, go through it all in detail—everything.'

She thought for a moment, and then embarked on her description; she spoke slowly, making a great effort to get the facts clear and correct and in their right order. Yet, as she progressed, both their faces became mystified, almost incredulous. There seemed to be nothing in Bellac's day of festival that was in any way remarkable. It started with a Mass, but then they always did, and it continued by way of food and drinks and presents for the children, through an afternoon of rustic games, too much wine and speeches, to an evening of dancing, fireworks, more wine, love in the shadows, more dancing, and yet again more wine.

There were embellishments, of course. There were processions, fancy dress, masks; the beautiful crucifix was taken from the church and carried round the village. Even Lindsay, with his slight knowledge of such things, could see that much which happened on Bellac's day of the Thirteen Days had its roots in the religions that flourished before Christ; but then everybody knew that the early Church had been much too wise to try to eradicate the ancient beliefs, preferring to incorporate them into her own ritual. There seemed to be nothing about Les Treize Jours to make it any more or less remarkable than a doll made of cornstalks perched on top of a haystack, or the choice of December 25th as Christmas Day.

And yet the fact remained that someone—either Philippe de Montfaucon himself or those who were willing to kill for him, but against his wishes—seemed to be determined that Lindsay should pass Les Treize Jours in a stupor.

As if to underline this suspicion there was a tap on the

door, and a maidservant came in carrying a steaming glass on a tray. Lindsay, who had been lying back on his pillows in any case, shut his eyes; but, from under lowered lids, he could see that the girl was a trifle taken aback to find her mistress in the room with him. She said, 'Dr. Chauvet said that the gentleman should have a little hot wine at six, madame.'

Françoise told her to put the wine on the table beside the bed. The maid seemed inclined to linger, but Françoise dismissed her. When she had gone Lindsay opened his eyes, and the two of them regarded the glass in silence.

'I'm sure,' Lindsay said at last, 'that we're on the right track. The idea is to keep me stoked up with Mère Blossac's knockout mixture. It's probably my fault for not promising your husband that I'd keep my nose out of things that don't concern me.'

Françoise picked up the glass, went to the window, and emptied the contents into the ivy which covered the castle wall; she stood for a moment gazing at the creeper as if expecting it to shrivel and die, but it had been there for a great many years —had probably had worse things poured on it in its time. 'Yes,' she said at last, 'it's crazy, but I think you're right. The point is what do we do about it?'

'We do nothing. I lie here and pretend to be in a coma.'

'Supposing ...' She shuddered. 'They tried to kill you— don't let's forget that.'

'They won't try again—not while I'm tucked up in bed, minding my own business.'

'You seem very sure of that.'

'*Philippe* was sure of it; I told you what he said. Don't you worry about me. I'm in the safest possible place.'

Yet when she had gone to say good night to her children and to dress for dinner, he felt suddenly very much alone and defenseless. The patch of sunlight on the wall turned from deep gold to a sullen red, and he found himself thinking again of the black tomb in the forest, of the bronze-green leaves chattering in the breeze and falling silent under the golden sky—of that song, disembodied, threatening, among the deepening shadows. Warm in his bed, he shuddered at the memory.

The sleeping draught was still at work in his veins; he kept sliding towards sleep, and jerking into wakefulness again; the questions that chased themselves endlessly round his brain became involved with snatches of dreams. The characters who posed the questions performed a round dance in and out of his dreaming and his waking—hand in hand, like the figures in a mediaeval frieze: Odile, with her amber eyes, and Prince Cottanero, the shadow of a virile man, and his pretty mistress Natasha, who did not in some way ring true. Hand in hand they passed, dancing: the boy, Christian, with his bow and arrow; the handsome, fleshy Abbé Luchard and his arrogant secretary; Père Dominique leading Philippe de Montfaucon in the dance; and always, among them or passing them, or waiting in the distance like background figures in a Breughel painting, the brown people of Bellac.

The waking moments brought odd flashes of intelligence. He thought suddenly that amid all this gallimaufrey of sleeping potions and dead white doves and old women who spat upon one in the road, it was strange that the name Cottanero should appear: *cotta nero*, the black surplice . . .

He struggled out of sleep to find two pink, solemn faces gazing into his own. After a moment he decided that they were not part of another dream. He heard Françoise say, 'They refused to go to bed until they'd seen you.'

Gilles and Antoinette nodded, round-eyed. Antoinette said, 'You hurt your forehead awfully, did you know?'

'Yes.'

Gilles said, '*I* fell off yesterday, too.'

'Were you jumping?' inquired the small girl. 'Jumping *is* rather difficult.'

Her mother said, 'I told you, darling; Uncle James's horse stumbled. Well, you've seen him. Now, how about bed?'

Gilles, ignoring this, sat down and peered earnestly into Lindsay's eyes. 'Was there much blood?'

'Masses.'

'Did you pass out?'

'Yes.'

'What's passing out like? Like having your tonsils out?'

Françoise said, 'That's quite enough. Uncle James isn't feeling at all well.'

Antoinette kissed him and Gilles shook hands with formality.

'Go on,' said Françoise. 'I'll come in a minute.'

The children trailed away, unwillingly. Something in the warm, nursery smell of them, the soft feel of their pajamas, had been very touching.

'They like you,' said Françoise. 'Isn't that a good thing?'

But before he could ask her what exactly she meant by this remark—and if, indeed, she meant what he hoped she did —she went on. 'James, they'll bring up some food presently; pretend to be asleep, don't eat it.'

'That's a bit hard—I'm ravenous.'

'I'll bring you something myself, later.' She hesitated, looking at him doubtfully. 'I hate leaving you all alone up here. Would you like old Rosalie, my maid, to sit with you?'

'I'd love it, but ... Well, if anyone wants to give me some more of Mother Blossac's mixture they've got to be able to— without suspecting anything.'

'You won't swallow it?'

'Not if I can help it. I'll fool them somehow.'

And yet, when the moment came, he found that it was easier said than done to fool them.

He had been dozing, only lightly, it seemed, because a faint rattle of the door handle woke him up. Some time before, he had turned on the light beside the bed, so that he was able to see the broad shoulders of Philippe's manservant as he turned from shutting the door—and, Lindsay suspected, locking it. The man was carrying a tray on which was a bowl of soup, bread, wine and fruit; but, by the way he put the tray down on the dressing table and not beside the bed, Lindsay guessed that food was not the main reason for his visit. He was lying on his side, face away from the light, and was thus able to watch all that happened without appearing to be awake.

The man took a bottle out of his pocket and poured the

contents of it into the wineglass; he then brought the whole tray to the bed. He said, quite loud, 'Your supper, monsieur.'

Lindsay continued to breathe heavily.

Louder: 'Your supper, monsieur.'

Since even this produced no response he bent over and tweaked Lindsay's ear. Lindsay continued to breathe stertorously, and curbed a desire to punch the man on the nose.

He now seemed to be satisfied that his patient was still comatose from the last dose. He rolled Lindsay onto his back and, using a large hand that smelled rather unpleasantly of Caporal cigarettes and garlic, forced his mouth open. Lindsay made the sort of noises that he imagined drugged sleepers made when subjected to such treatment; he only just had time to seal his throat, by contracting the muscles, before he felt the liquid splashing onto his tongue. Luckily there was not more than a couple of tablespoonfuls, and he could close his mouth on it with ease. He gave an imitation gulp and was relieved to find that only a trickle of the stuff got past his constricted throat; it tasted absolutely filthy, and he immediately recognized it as the same concoction which the old woman had given him the previous night.

The man seemed to take an age unlocking the door and leaving the room. As soon as he had gone, Lindsay spat the mixture back into the glass, and then poured it into the carafe of wine; he hoped that the man himself might drink it when the tray finally found its way back to the kitchen quarters. He wondered what would have happened if he had been awake. A taste of the soup gave him the answer; they were certainly taking no chances.

Now, lying in the silent room, he could hear the sounds of voices and laughter from the terrace. He remembered that Françoise had said that there would be a large party on the eve of Les Treize Jours; he tried to imagine what other, even more curious guests might have joined those he already knew, but this flight of the imagination led him again into sleep.

This must have been the deep slumber of exhaustion, his system beginning to escape from the drug, for when Françoise finally came to him with her maid and a tray of food, he refused it and turned over to sleep again. She kissed him and withdrew.

Later still, other figures moved in the shadows of the room. Old Mère Blossac crept forward to listen to his breathing, to put one wise finger, light as a dry, dead leaf, on the pulse in his wrist. After she had gone Philippe de Montfaucon stood beside the bed for a long time, looking down at the sleeping face with affection and compassion. He only moved when Father Dominique joined him, touching him lightly on the shoulder.

When Lindsay finally awoke, he found that his head was clear; he found also that Françoise was standing by the bed in a dressing gown. The look on her face, revealed by the first chill light of dawn, made him sit up with a gasp of fear, sleep falling from him with the bedclothes.

He said, 'Françoise! For God's sake . . .'

She put her hands—those long delicate hands—over her face. 'It's Gilles,' she said. 'My baby.'

'What . . . ?'

She removed the hands, and stared at him. He was out of bed by now, putting on his dressing gown, only a little surprised to find that he was hardly dizzy at all. He took her by the shoulders, holding her firmly, and at his touch she seemed to grow calmer.

'I don't know why I woke up,' she said. 'Mothers do have this sort of . . . intuition. I went straight to the nursery, but I . . . It sounds impossible, but I knew, James, before I got there. He wasn't in his bed.'

'I'll get dressed; we'll look for him.'

He had already turned towards his clothes before she said, 'No. I know where he is.'

Lindsay turned back.

'He's in the chapel—with Philippe.'

He stared, amazed.

'Yes, I know; it's lunatic, isn't it? Five o'clock in the morning! God knows how long he's been there; his bed's quite cold.'

Lindsay was angry suddenly, and, angry, he wanted action.

'This is absurd,' he said. 'You've got your key; let's go and ...'

Françoise was shaking her head. 'The key's no good. Some-one must have found out; the door's nailed up from inside. I ... Oh James, I heard his voice—that's all.'

They stared at each other, almost unbelievingly, while the light grew stronger around them. Outside, a cockerel began to crow, welcoming the day—welcoming Bellac's Day of the Thirteen Days.

II

The Twelve Dancers

It was as though, suddenly, out of a mist of question and surmise and suspicion, they had stumbled upon reality; and yet the reality was like a smooth pinnacle of rock upon which they could gain no hold.

The nursery maid was lying. She stood with her back to the door in her mistress's blue-and-gold sitting room, and lied, and lied. She had slept very soundly—she always slept soundly. If the boy had left his bed during the night she knew nothing of it; all that she knew was that he had been there fast asleep when she had waked up. It was all plausible and all untrue; her eyes, the pose of her whole body gave her away.

But this was nothing. It was the small boy himself who took their breath away. He had had a dream, he said—a dream about Gogo, his pony; Gogo was ill, Gogo was dying; and so he had got out of bed and gone down to the stable. Yes, he had stayed down there a long time; as a matter of fact he had fallen asleep down there.

The horrifying thing about this recital was not so much that he lied, not so much that he told so plausible a story (because he had obviously been taught it), but that—unlike the nursery maid—he lied so beautifully. Only the agony that was revealed in his mother's face prevented Lindsay from believing every word of it.

And yet the child lying because he had been told to, and the maid lying because she was afraid of losing her job, might have been bearable; it was the groom who took the whole thing out of the realms of the nursery and into a world of organized adult conspiracy. Oh yes, he said, certainly the boy had come down to the stable in the middle of night. What time? Well, that was hard to say, but somewhere around four perhaps. Scared stiff he had been—some tale about his pony being ill; and nothing would satisfy him except that he must sit in the stall with the pony. Fallen asleep in the stall, he had. Why, it was pretty to see.

Françoise and Lindsay faced each other across the elegant sunlit room. Nightmare had emerged from the shadows and now walked with them in daylight.

Outside on the terrace and downstairs in the hall, there was a crush of people; every minute cars were arriving, voices were raised in greeting. This was Bellac's day, and the neighbors of Bellac meant to make the most of it. Golden sunlight carpeted the valley. Even the dark bluff above the shimmering lake had clothed itself in a haze of heat that softened its harsh contours and the dull, dead green of conifer and yew and ivy. The mountains were merely a blue shadow on the horizon.

All Bellac smiled; all Bellac's guests laughed and chattered and drank their host's very excellent chilled white wine. From the village came the sound of bells and the distant oom-pa of a brass band. Bellac was en fête. In the small blue-and-gold sitting room Lindsay and Françoise stared at each other, lost for words, seeking in each other's eyes a reassurance which neither could give.

The little clock on the mantelpiece chimed eleven o'clock. Françoise glanced out of the window. Already, across the lawns and down the side of the formal garden, there was a movement of guests towards the village. She said, 'It's time for Mass. Oh James, I can't; I can't face it.'

He went over to her and put his arms round her, holding her tightly. 'You must,' he said.

'He's never lied to me before. I can't bear it.'

He thought it better to ignore this. 'You must go, because if you don't it'll be so obvious that you know something—something which they're very keen to keep secret.'

She swung away from him angrily. 'They, they! Who, James?'

'They.' He repeated it musingly. 'We don't know who, yet.'

Françoise stood at the window, looking out, glaring out. 'Why not all of them?' she asked bitterly. 'Isn't that what you feel? All of them—against us.'

Her maid tapped on the door and came in apologetically. 'It's time, madame,' she said. 'Monsieur le Marquis and the children have started.'

Françoise nodded absently.

When the woman had gone Lindsay said, 'I imagine someone's already had a nasty shock to find that I wasn't in bed and comatose this morning; if, on top of that, you don't appear at the church . . .'

'Yes, you're right. What about you?'

He suddenly thought how absurd this was; how ridiculous that they should be talking to each other like conspirators —like members of a resistance movement—on this bright morning with the calm note of the bell calling them to Mass across sunlit lake and meadows.

'I'll be there,' he said. 'But I think I'll keep well out of the way.'

Françoise still hesitated, smoothing her immaculate gloves nervously. 'I hate him for this,' she said. 'I'm horrified to find how much I hate him.'

Lindsay nodded. 'I understand that; and yet somehow I feel that he . . . he doesn't deserve hatred.'

She did not reply, but crossed the room, kissed his cheek, and went to the door; she paused there, looking back. 'Such a lovely day,' she said, 'and I feel as if I were going out into a fog. What's going to happen, James?'

He spread his hands. 'I wish I knew.'

Upstairs in her barricaded apartment, Tante Estelle said to

her maid, Marianne, 'Get out my gray hat. I've decided to go to Mass after all.'

Lindsay was rather surprised by the large number of people still left in the great hall of the castle when he finally went downstairs. In the village the churchbell was still tolling. As he looked at the assembly, standing round talking very loudly and all at once with glasses in their hands, it struck him that the sound was more like an interval bell in a theater than a call to worship.

He saw Natasha standing by herself, beautifully posed against a piece of tapestry as if waiting for a photographer; he joined her, hoping that she might be able to bring him up-to-date on his knowledge of Bellac's guests.

'They can't all be staying here,' he said.

Natasha's large eyes widened. 'Oh *no*!' From the horrified tone of her voice he gathered that possibly those who *were* staying had been enough for her. Yet, when he pressed her for details, she seemed curiously at a loss to point out anyone of interest. He received an impression that a natural curiosity, a natural love of scandal was warring inside her with a far from natural discretion; not for the first time he found himself wondering exactly what did go on behind locked doors when she had retired with her prince for the night. There was no doubt at all that she had been told to keep her mouth shut when talking to the Englishman. A moment later Cottanero himself confirmed these suspicions by swooping down on them and bearing her away to church without so much as a glance at Lindsay.

He wondered whether Betty, Comtesse de Vignon, might prove more communicative.

Walking down to the village with her, he realized that she, like himself, like Françoise, was an outsider; he was becoming increasingly aware that at Bellac on this Day of the Thirteen Days the guests were sharply divided into those who knew what was afoot and those who did not. The Countess Betty was full of information, but it was blind information; he had to make of it what he could.

'Between you and me,' she said, in a whisper that might have carried half a mile on a quiet day, 'both English, you know, and all that, where in heaven's name do Philippe and Françoise get such a crew *from*?'

'Odd?' Lindsay suggested.

'*Odd!*' she snorted. 'They're a damn lot of cranks, half of 'em.'

He wondered whether this merely meant that they found other things more interesting than horses. 'My dear,' she was saying, 'it takes a lot to frighten me, but there's one feller—Polish, I gather, wonderful war record and so on, face all cut to pieces—he doesn't open his mouth; hasn't said a word, as far as I can see, since he arrived last night. Titled, too; ought to know better. I tell you, my friend, I'll be damn glad to get away from the place. I mean to say, I'm fond of Philippe and Françoise, no nonsense about them; wouldn't be about a man who could breed horses like he does. But some of their guests!'

Lindsay was interested. 'You're going then?'

'My dear, of course I am. Women definitely not required after today. I can't think why not, I bet I'm as good a shot as any of that lot; however—apparently it's a tradition. After Les Treize Jours the men have a jolly good booze-up and go hunting during the day. Though why the French call shooting 'hunting' I'll never know. Tried to get Françoise to come to my place for a few days, but she wouldn't. Must be deathly dull for her—only that mad old aunt to talk to . . .'

Lindsay let her ramble on. He realized that he himself had progressed beyond the point where what she said was of any interest at all. The night that had passed had been a turning point; the time of conjecture was over; now, soon, revelation would begin. The woman beside him, irritated, disturbed by something she could only just sense, belonged to another world; whereas he . . . he was beginning to understand something of the meaning of the shapes in the darkness.

He managed to elude her in the crowds that were moving along the little streets of the village; instinctively he knew that his place on this day was among the simple (or was that the word?) people of Bellac.

Everywhere he looked there were flags, posies of flowers, thick garlands of evergreen. In the square the several hundred people who had been unable to find room in the church itself were sharing in the Mass, somewhat vicariously, through the good graces of a rather ancient loudspeaker which had been rigged up over the door. Under the green shade of the plane trees, trestle tables were laid with great flagons of wine, with boards bearing cartwheels of the flat local cheese, huge dark red hams which had been smoking all the year in pungent chimneys; there were dishes of olives and short, fat cucumbers, sheaves of long loaves, a small mountain of dark green melons, a shroud of white muslin that covered row upon row of open tarts filled with apple or plum or apricot. A small crowd of children stood in front of two vast wine barrels, draped with bunting and filled with sawdust, out of which would eventually emerge their presents. The band, their uniform jackets unbuttoned to expose sweaty chests, were already broaching the wine, presumably to recompense themselves in advance for the dry hours of puffing and blowing which were to come.

Standing well back in the shadow of the plane trees, Lindsay found it hard to believe that anything lay beneath the jolly, ordinary surface of the day, let alone anything sinister. Watching the brown country faces as they listened to the Mass or gossiped quietly in corners or admonished the darting children, he could find nothing which he had not seen a hundred times before: the young men in their best shirts and trousers eyeing those girls who were not in church, and the girls pretending that they were unaware of the eyes, yet each already planning how to appropriate this or that young man, and the old people withdrawn, remembering other summers, and the children simply excited and impatient beyond endurance for the fun to begin—these were the same all over the world.

Birds quarreled in the plane trees; wasps gathered about the wine; the ancient liturgy droned on, blurred a little by the age of the loudspeaker. There was not, there could not be, a mystery behind all this. And yet, if his suspicions were right, there was something here of such importance that he had been brutally drugged in order that he should not witness it.

Suddenly his pulse quickened; he had seen a face. Yes, there on the other side of the square was Christian; he was pausing to talk to some local people, and there was something in his attitude toward them as well as in theirs toward him which Lindsay could not quite grasp: a kind of ... What? Almost a kinship. Certainly an easier, altogether more intimate reciprocity than he would have expected.

Laughing, the boy dodged past one of the men beside the trestle tables, stole a peach from a golden pile of them and ran out into the sunlight. And then an odd thing happened.

The people began to boo him, to jeer at him, to shout out names which were at one and the same time insulting and friendly—in much the same way that the word *bastard* in English can be almost a term of endearment.

The boy crossed the square, laughing, and this ripple of mockery, of what Lindsay could only define as mock mockery, followed him—followed him until he was lost to view.

Lindsay had no time to wonder at this extraordinary incident because immediately following it there was a flurry of movement; people began to move towards the church. After a moment the figure of Père Dominique appeared in the doorway; he came out and stood in the middle of the path—just where the three Montfaucons of long ago had chosen to be laid to rest. Lindsay's first thought was that he would give the blessing to those outside, but in this he was wrong; he began to speak the opening verses of one of the Gospels, Lindsay was unsure which:

'"In the beginning was the Word, and the Word was with God, and the Word was God. The same was in the beginning with God ..."'

Now, Lindsay knew that his nerves were on edge—that he was standing there only to find whatever was strange or untoward in what he witnessed; yet he was totally unprepared for the impact which these well-known words had upon the people around him. A silence fell that was so profound that it even affected the children, even (he could have sworn it) the birds. And was it his imagination, or had a kind of electric spark of anticipation run through the crowd? He thought that faces which a minute ago had been relaxed, even drowsy in the murmurous heat of midday, were now sharp, attentive to the point of . . . Yes, almost to the point of fear.

'". . . He was in the world, and the world was made by Him, and the world knew Him not . . ."' The priest's voice droned on.

Quite suddenly Lindsay was afraid. The spark of emotion in the people around him became too strong; it leaped the space between his body and theirs and transfixed him.

'". . . But as many as received Him, to them gave He power to become the sons of God . . ."'

Only later would he be able to understand the meaning of the words—or rather the meaning they had for this poised, utterly silent crowd; at this moment he was so much a part of them that he only felt the excitement, the hysteria, and it was utterly unnerving because it was soundless—the hysteria of a yelling mob was easy to understand; what he experienced here was not.

Now the priest was moving down the steep slope from the little church. Behind him people were streaming out of the doorway. Lindsay found that the square, which had a moment ago seemed spacious, was suddenly packed to suffocation; in that clenched silence he had a shrill desire to cry out, but he realized that his mouth was too dry to accommodate him, even if he had been able to find the strength of will to oppose the mass will which gripped him.

'". . . not of blood, nor of the will of the flesh, nor of the will of man, but of God."'

Now even that one voice was silent. Lindsay was aware of the thudding of his own heart; but it was the sound that broke the silence which really struck terror into him: a man began to sing, and not only the song but the voice that sang it were known to him; he had last heard them as he stood undecided by the black-marble gravestone in the darkening forest.

There was another surge of movement in the crowd; for a moment his view was obscured, and when he could see again, there were the dancers.

Perhaps Françoise had not described them very well, or perhaps he himself, not knowing for what he searched in her description, had ignored the important details; he knew, before he counted them, that there were twelve. It was a moment before he noticed the thirteenth figure, which did not dance; the thirteenth man was the singer, and he wore a golden half-mask which was not quite human, not quite animal. He walked slowly, singing, and his twelve companions, also masked, circled round him; there was no abandon in the dance and no jollity; these men, in their masks and dark-green tabards, were performing a solemn act of worship.

The two numbers, twelve and thirteen, were performing leap-frog in Lindsay's brain; the two ideas—no, they were less ideas than certainties—occurred at the same moment. Les Treize Jours, he thought. The thirteen days which were so absurd because they were one day. *Jours . . . Joueurs.* Of course that was it—not *jours*, meaning *days*, but *joueurs*, meaning *players*, meaning *performers*. The day took its name from the thirteen men gyrating so solemnly in the square before him, watched in such a tense, anticipatory silence by the people of the valley. And the other thought, reaching out to him from that slab of black marble in the forest, was: 'The Twelve dance on high, Amen. The Whole on high hath part in our dancing. Amen. Whoso danceth not, knoweth not what cometh to pass. Amen.'

His brain reeled; he was aware that a hundred things which had mystified him were now tugging at the edges of his understanding.

But all these rioting thoughts and discoveries were swept out of his mind by what happened next. He was aware that the singing had stopped, as abruptly as it had begun; the dancers were standing perfectly still, looking away from him. He realized that the center of interest—of this passionate absorption—had shifted; all heads had turned as if blown by the same gust of wind. Craning, he caught a glimpse of Philippe de Montfaucon at the edge of the crowd; he seemed to be bending down. He thought he saw Francoise, her face very white. A second later Philippe straightened up. Lindsay saw that he was holding his young son in the crook of his arm; his breath caught in his throat.

Yet the words which the Marquis de Bellac spoke were so mundane, so anticlimactic, that Lindsay nearly laughed out loud—nearly missed the whole point of all that he had seen.

'Welcome, all of you, to Bellac and to Les Treize Jours.'

Then Philippe inclined his head, looked down at his son —and kissed him lightly.

The vast, communal gasp of the crowd came at exactly the same moment as the woman's scream; in Lindsay's mind they were indivisible.

He caught the shrill words: 'No. Ah dear God, no ...' And he glimpsed the white distraught face of Tante Estelle as she crumpled, fluttering, into the dust.

The banging on the door echoed down the long passage that led to Tante Estelle's preposterously overcrowded sitting room; it reverberated among the chimes of the grandfather clock and caused the lusters of the dusty chandelier to tinkle delicately.

The old woman lay on a chaise longue, her face pale, almost transparent against the red cushions; her eyes, however, were very bright, possibly even vindictive. Lindsay, Françoise and the sturdy red-faced maid, Marianne, were all looking towards the door, as if expecting it to give way at any minute before that thunderous knocking.

After a moment the knocking stopped, and Philippe de Montfaucon's voice shouted, 'Marianne, open the door. Open this door at once.'

Tante Estelle turned her head among the cushions; her voice was faint, shadowy: 'Speak to him, Marianne. Don't let him in.'

Marianne gestured curtly to Lindsay to stand out of the line of the passage; she then squared her formidable shoulders and advanced to the fray. Before unbolting the door, however, she slipped a heavy chain into its socket.

In the room they heard the bolts clatter back, heard the big lock snap open. At once Philippe must have thrust his weight at the door, but the chain outwitted him, leaving only a gap of some two inches.

They heard him say, 'Let me in, woman; I've got to talk to your mistress.'

Marianne said, 'Mademoiselle has taken a tisane and a sleeping draught. She is already asleep.'

'Then wake her at once.'

'That, Monsieur le Marquis, I cannot do ...'

'You'll do as I say.'

'Forgive me, Monsieur le Marquis, but I am a working woman, and I am no longer young. I would remind monsieur that it is Mademoiselle who pays my wages; it is more than my job is worth to disobey her orders.'

They heard the rustle of banknotes, and Marianne's voice very genuinely aggrieved: 'Monsieur, there is also loyalty.'

'Very well.' Not even Philippe could disguise the boiling rage behind the reasonable tone. 'Very well. It will not transgress your code of loyalty, I feel sure, to tell me whether Madame la Marquise is with my aunt.'

'Mademoiselle is alone.'

'Neither she nor M. Lindsay?'

'Mademoiselle is alone; she is asleep.'

After a moment there was the sound of the bolts being shot home, of the ancient lock clacking into place again. Marianne returned, nodded grimly to her mistress, ignoring Françoise and Lindsay, and left the room.

For a long time there was silence. A bee was bumbling about among the layers of frilled lace curtains that covered the windows. The old woman's eyes were closed; she might have been asleep—or dead—in this dusty sepulcher of a forgotten past.

After a time she gave a sigh—a deep, weary sigh that

seemed to come up out of her very soul. They did not know it then, but this was a sigh of capitulation; there was remorse in it, and there was release in it.

'Philippe is afraid,' she said. 'Afraid of what I am going to tell you.' She had not opened her eyes. 'It has been a secret between us for so long—just between the two of us.' She smiled faintly. 'It is amusing that now he should be afraid of me—when for so many years I have been afraid of him—afraid that *he* might tell it.'

Neither Lindsay nor Françoise spoke; it was as if they both held their breath. Tante Estelle, still without opening her eyes, said, 'I knew, you see, as soon as you—' she gestured vaguely towards Lindsay—'spoke to me of death—of Philippe being afraid of death.'

Again she was silent; then she turned her head on the cushions—turned it restlessly to and fro. 'Or did I know before that? One lies to oneself. It is a sin. When I saw the boy, I knew.'

Françoise said, 'Christian?'

Tante Estelle nodded. 'Christian. The other was called ... How one's memory betrays one! Was it Armand? Yes, I think it was Armand.'

Lindsay and Françoise exchanged a look. Françoise said, 'The other one?'

'Long ago. Why did I stay here? To see it happen again? Bah, I must be mad.'

Suddenly she opened her eyes and looked at them—first at Lindsay, then at her niece by marriage. 'I suppose he's your lover,' she said. 'Oh, *I* don't blame you; there's a lot to be said for lovers, even I know it. Besides that happened before, too.'

Françoise knelt beside the chaise longue. 'My dear, what happened before? Who was Armand?'

Tante Estelle touched the younger woman's smooth face with a gentle old finger. 'Your children are like we were: just like Alain and me. You never met Alain, did you? My darling brother, Philippe's father.'

'He was drowned long before I was married, you know that.'

'I don't know what I know; that's the truth. Alain and I were so close—just like your Gilles, your Antoinette. Gilles is the image of Alain; perhaps that's why I love him so much—why I am going to tell you what I swore . . . Yes, I swore it on the Holy Bible. I swore never to speak of it to a living soul.'

Suddenly she put her hands up to her face, pressing her white cheeks so hard that the imprint of the fingers stayed there long after the hands had dropped to her lap again.

'I swore on the Bible, so I am damned; but then perhaps I am damned in any case. But when I saw Philippe lift up his son and kiss him . . . Did I cry out? I can't remember. When I saw it, I was a child again; I was looking up at my father as he lifted my darling brother—down there in the square, on this same day, all those years ago . . .' She shook her head as if to dispel that confusion in time which haunted her.

Lindsay could contain himself no longer. 'You know the meaning of it then? Of the dancers, and the tomb in the forest —your own father's tomb—and Philippe's fear of death?'

Tante Estelle stared at him, her eyes wide yet curiously vacant. After a moment she shook her head. 'I know nothing,' she repeated, 'except that I saw it all before. I didn't understand it then, and I don't understand it now. But my father . . . Yes, there was a young man, Armand. My father—' she glanced at Françoise—'turned from my mother. She was not as strong as you are—not as good as you are; she went away; she made a fool of herself with many men.'

Lindsay could feel the excitement dying inside him. He had thought that here, locked in this muddled old brain, were the answers to all the questions that taunted him; but, as she herself had said, she knew nothing—well, perhaps a little more than he had suspected, that was all. Was it only a desire to prevent the old lady telling them this—these feeble memories of a dead past—that had brought Philippe de Montfaucon banging at her door like a madman? He could have spared himself the trouble.

But Françoise, more reasonable, more patient, was saying, 'Darling, tell us; you must tell us now—what was it that you swore to keep to yourself?'

The old woman nodded. 'Yes, I must tell you. For your little boy, you see, because I love him so much. Will God forgive me? For the love of a child, will He forgive me?'

Gently Françoise said, 'I think He will.'

Tante Estelle looked at Lindsay. 'I don't know the answers to your questions—because I am a woman, and this is a man's secret. You are a man; you can save Gilles—perhaps you can save Philippe as well, I don't know about that; but you can save Gilles—he doesn't have to go the same way as my own dear brother.'

Lindsay took a step nearer to her. Françoise was holding the thin dry hand; she said, 'You mean ... I always suspected it. Philippe's father wasn't drowned by accident; he committed suicide to escape from something?'

Tante Estelle shook her head, never taking her eyes off Lindsay.

Françoise said, 'It really *was* an accident then?'

Still looking at Lindsay, the old woman said, 'Neither an accident, nor suicide; it was a plan. He is still alive.'

12

The Drowned Man

The church clock in the Old Town of Hyères was striking midnight as Lindsay climbed out of the Renault. He had been driving for six hours. He was tired and stiff, and his wounded forehead was aching abominably; yet during that drive he had become aware of a feeling of desperate urgency. He could not say how it had started, or what combination of circumstances had given birth to it; all he knew was that he could not banish from his mind a picture of Françoise—of her face as she had watched him drive away, pale, drawn, her eyes smudged with violet shadows of anxiety and fatigue.

The last thing he felt like doing was broaching an unknown old man of uncertain temper, particularly when he knew that his very presence here meant that a closely guarded secret had been betrayed. And this, moreover, at midnight.

He left the car in the ancient, paved square and went into a café. Clearly the tourists, whose cars had made the greater part of his journey a nightmare, never penetrated to the Old Town of Hyères—at any rate not in the evenings; the handful of local men who looked up as he entered did not seem unduly grateful for the pleasure of his company, though they did express some interest at the speed with which he dispatched four glasses of brandy and a cup of scalding-hot black coffee.

Following their directions he found the Villa Oriflamme without difficulty; he stood for some time, looking at the heavy wooden door set in the high wall and rubbing his chin. The noise of the bell, when he did finally pull the iron ring which operated it, scared him out of his wits—also half the dogs in the neighborhood; and he was surprised by the speed with which this tintinnabulation was answered. The door opened, and he found himself staring into the eyes of one of the most murderous-looking Arabs he had ever seen. This individual, however, seemed to be impressed by the letter which Tante Estelle had given to Lindsay as a passport, and on the back of which she had written her name with a bold flourish. He bowed, opened the door a little wider and stood to one side.

Lindsay found himself in a courtyard with a mimosa growing in the center of it. The Arab closed the gate, gave Lindsay a small secret smile which was far from reassuring and vanished into the house. Lindsay sat down on a stone seat, still, at this late hour, slightly warm from the day's sun, and waited.

He waited a long time. Presently the Arab reappeared and ushered him into the villa—or rather through it—to a vine-hung terrace. There was still no sign of the man who had once been called Alain de Montfaucon, Marquis de Bellac, but who now called himself M. Alain Gravier. Lindsay realized that the letter must have been a great shock to him; a secret which had for many years been in the possession of only two people, and those two people immediate blood relations, had now, for all that the old man knew, become the property of the whole wide world.

The terrace was perched high up on a little cliff; it seemed to have been hewn out of the rock or out of the thick walls of the Old Town. Below it was a jumble of brown roofs, the tower of the church, the twinkling windows of Hyères, and, in the distance, the lights of the plage and a half-moon reflected in the Mediterranean. Gazing at this view Lindsay did not hear the step behind him; only when something white moved into his field of vision did he turn abruptly. He found himself looking at a massive nurse wearing a uniform and an aggrieved expression. Her voice was English and genteel. 'You *have* upset M. Gravier, young man; it's a great pity. Still it's done now, and he insists on coming down.'

Lindsay said, 'I'm sorry; I . . . I didn't realize that he was ill.'

'He isn't,' replied the nurse, and added darkly, 'at the moment. We have enough trouble when Mlle. de Montfaucon comes to stay here once a year, without . . . Oh well.' She began to puff up the cushions on the terrace chairs. 'As I say to M. Gravier, "You and your old flames—at your age!" He likes a little joke, you know.'

There was something both grotesque and tragic in this— the old lady having to visit the brother she loved so much in the guise of an 'old flame.'

'Ah,' the nurse said, 'here he comes. Now you be careful, young man, won't you?' And she put one finger to her head with the ghastly callousness of her kind. 'Not badly,' she added. 'But we just take care.'

'Take care of what?' inquired a querulous voice from the darkness of the room behind them, also speaking in English.

'Of this terrace,' she replied brightly, 'and we don't go sitting on the parapet like this young visitor of yours.'

'Oh, go away, you stupid woman,' said Philippe's father as he came into view seated in a wheelchair which was being pushed by the Arab. 'And shut these windows—all of them; there are times when I demand to be private.'

He had a long, narrow head and the kind of distinguished

features associated with diplomats of the old school or with prelates in port advertisements; Lindsay thought that in the elegant, high-stiff-collared and long-narrow-trousered days of his youth he would have been accounted a very handsome man. But he had clearly had a stroke, which probably explained the wheelchair; two spots of unhealthily high color burned on the fine cheekbones—Philippe's cheekbones.

'I suppose,' he said, speaking in French now, 'that fearful woman has been telling you I'm off my head?'

'She hinted as much.'

The old man nodded. 'Well,' he said, 'maybe I am; I sometimes think ninety-nine per cent of the world is.'

Then he was silent, his dark eyes—Montfaucon eyes, as Lindsay knew from his study of the family portraits—fixed on the young man before him. Looking into them, Lindsay thought, Yes, he could well be deranged, and yet . . .

The old voice broke in on his thoughts. 'I am ashamed to think what your opinion of our family must be.' He leaned forward. 'I'm a proud man; it hurts me to say that. Do you understand—it hurts me?'

The eyes were indeed remarkable. Lindsay noticed now that the stroke had twisted the face a little. 'I understand,' he said.

A light gust of wind came off the sea and set the single overhead lantern that lit the terrace swinging a little; the shifting shadows on the old man's face made it look as though he were under water. 'Would it be surprising,' he asked, 'if I *was* mad? Dear God, aren't they all mad? Haven't the Montfaucons been mad since time immemorial?' He laughed suddenly—a laugh made mirthless by his false teeth. 'You *could* say that I'm the only sane one.' He shook his head, as if this was something he didn't believe himself. 'You could say that *they* were the only sane ones, and the rest of the world mad. It doesn't matter, it doesn't matter.'

There was a knock on the French windows behind them; the nurse appeared with a shawl which she put round her patient's thin shoulders.

'The only good thing about her,' he said, 'is that she can't understand French, and never will.'

Then, for a long time, he was silent. The little gusts of wind came and went; the lantern swung; the leaves of the vine whispered; the lights of Hyères twinkled far below.

When the old voice spoke again it was entirely changed. Any assurance it had possessed, any élan, had vanished completely; it was a shadow of a voice, and Lindsay understood, suddenly, what life had been for this old man. The voice was shadowy because it was the voice of a shadow—of a man who had lost his identity, only to find that he could not assume another.

'I've never even seen my grandson,' he said, almost to himself. 'Nor my daughter-in-law, come to that. They say she's a beauty.' He looked up, and the old eyes were weary, almost puzzled. 'There are times when I almost feel that I really did drown that day at Antibes. "No," I have to tell myself, "you swam round the headland, and the car was waiting . . ." ' His voice trailed away; he shook his head and sighed.

Lindsay said, 'But why? Why did you have to do it?'

The old man stared at him for a moment; then he chuckled but without very much amusement. 'I pretended to die,' he said, 'because I was afraid of dying; and the result is that I'm dead. Or might as well be. Sounds like one of those Bellac riddles, doesn't it? "Whoso danceth not, knoweth not what cometh to pass" and all the rest of it?'

He noticed the way that Lindsay's head jerked up at these words, and again he gave that dry rasp of mirth.

When he next spoke his voice had changed yet again; it sounded almost impatient, bored.

'My sister writes that you will save the child; she says you are a good man, brave . . . Everything I am not.' He held up a bony, frail hand to stop Lindsay speaking. 'You can only do this if you know what it is that you are saving him from. But what I can tell you is only a little; they never trusted me, I was never perfect, all that I *know* is only a little—and much of what I know I have forgotten.'

He shook his head, the bowed, white-haired figure in the shawl, strangely lit by the swinging lantern. 'No. Even that is not true. I have forgotten nothing, but I am ... afraid to speak; there are things I dare not tell.'

Again he was silent. Lindsay felt that impatience, that sense of precious time wasted, nagging at the edges of his mind.

The old man said, 'Is Cottanero there? Luchard?'

'Yes.' He was surprised; the impatience vanished. 'Do you know them?'

'No man knows them; no man knows any of them, but they know each other. What is the date?'

Lindsay stared. The old voice was querulous again. 'The date, boy, the date, the day of the month?'

'It's the thirty-first of July—or rather ... No, because it's after midnight: the first of August.'

The old man sat up suddenly. 'August,' he said. 'Already! Then my son ...' He broke off; he did, at this moment, look quite insane. Lindsay felt fear tingle in his spine.

'Your son?'

But the other shook his head, staring vacantly. 'It doesn't matter,' he said again. 'It doesn't matter. We are neither of us God. How shall I tell you this? What do you already know ...?'

And suddenly he began to talk. As if a floodgate in his brain had been opened, the turbulent waters of memory came gushing out, sweeping everything before them in a torrent of history, folklore, superstition and death. There was no order in what he said: he spoke of the ancient religion—of the dance around the standing stone, the stone that was the phallus of all the world, the dance that would make all the world fruitful; he spoke of the twin gods of the Persians—the god of Light forever at war with the god of Darkness, and the world forever torn between them; he spoke of the Persian Mithra, whose origins were lost beyond the horizons of time—and of how Mithra was born in a cave on what is now called the twenty-fifth of December, of how he was worshipped by shepherds, of how he killed the bull and gave life to the earth; he spoke of the eternal principles of numbers, and of how the number four will always return to unity, which is God, because one plus two plus three plus four equals ten which equals one, ad infinitum.

Lindsay, staring, leaning forward in his chair and, staring, was appalled by the sense which these apparently unrelated maunderings, spoken by a man who might or who might not be in control of his faculties, made in his mind when related to Bellac.

And still the frail voice, the hollow voice, went on. He told of how the Romans had brought the god Mithra into France: the god who was a god of soldiers, a god of men—of men without women; and he spoke also of the ancients, to whom the love of man for man was pure love, while the love of man for woman was not.

Sometimes the words were, to Lindsay, meaningless; there were phrases which eluded him even as he grasped at them: '... the Seven Powers ... The Eighth Heaven ... the Soldier, the Raven, the Persian, the Lion ...' Twice he tried to stop the voice, to question it, but the old man could not or would not stop.

He began now to tell of Christ, and of how, to the men of His time and of the centuries immediately after Him, there was little difference between His teaching and the teaching of the prophets who had preceded Him. Had not Christ stood for Good against Evil in the endless struggle between them for the possession of the soul of man? So had Mithra.

And now, Lindsay knew, they had reached the heart of the matter. When the old voice told of the early heresies of the Church, he felt a thrill of recognition: the Stoics, the Gnostics, the Cathars. For there had been men who were both Christians *and* pagans, who argued that if God was Love how then could He have created a world so dark and sinful? The world of the flesh, of lust and greed and envy, was the world of evil; the world of the spirit was the world of God, and the two worlds were forever at war in the souls of men.

'Do you begin to see?' said the old man at last. 'The ancient religion did not die with the coming of Christ; His teaching only strengthened it, as had the teaching of many other prophets. The old beliefs only died when the Christian Church killed them—because it would tolerate no rival; and even then they still survived in what you would now call an underground movement. Witchcraft was not evil until the Christians named it so; it had not been evil for thousand upon thousand of years; it was only the most primitive belief—the dance round the standing stone that would make the earth fertile; it still exists, everywhere; it must, because that is how life is created.'

'And,' said Lindsay, 'at Bellac?'

Philippe's father bowed his head. Again, for what seemed a long time, he was silent. 'I did not mean to defend my people,' he said, 'but I find that I am—and this is strange, because I hate them; they destroyed my life; they made me . . .' He spread his hands. '. . . this.'

He shook his head sadly. 'Bellac,' he said. 'How I miss it!'

A stronger gust of wind rattled the wooden shutters of the house. The old man looked up at the lantern.

'These religions,' he said, 'which the Church called heresies because they deified the idea of evil as well as the idea of good . . . These religions were persecuted; thousands of honest and sincere men were massacred in the name of Christ. Well, there's nothing new in that. Languedoc, in fact all Southern France, suffered more than any other region. The Troubadours, as you may know, came from Languedoc, and the songs they sang—as you probably don't know—were nothing to do with the love of knights for fair ladies; they were hymns of the old religion, and any physical love they extolled had nothing to do with women, for, you see, the love of man for woman was of the flesh, evil: to bring more souls into a world ruled by evil was, in itself, a sin . . .'

The dark eyes were very bright. 'You see?'

'Yes. I see,' said Lindsay—thinking of Philippe and Christian.

'But persecution and massacre could not kill the old beliefs. When have they ever killed beliefs? They lived on in secret—yes, even in England. The Grail, before it became holy, held the ancient secret of Mithra. The old beliefs took refuge in legends—and in mountains, and ... in valleys.'

Again their eyes met.

'Christianity could absorb the old religion, making Mithra's birthday the official birthday of Christ, making the Grail holy; but the old religion could also absorb Christianity. They have never been true Christians in the valley of Bellac; when Père Dominique celebrates Mass, the words that the people hear are not the same words that you hear ...'

'But,' said Lindsay, 'that means ...' He broke off, staggered by his own thoughts. 'It means that Père Dominique is the center of the whole thing; he is the man who keeps it alive.'

'He is not alone. You must understand that in the great schools of the church ...' He crossed himself and shook his head. 'I am old,' he said. 'I must watch my tongue. But yes, you are right; at Bellac, Père Dominique is a man of great power—and beyond Bellac too.'

Lindsay was remembering how he had watched the Abbé Luchard meeting this man: remembering how surprised he had been to see the deference which that wealthy and sophisticated man of the world had shown to the shabby parish priest. He realized now that in the secret hierarchy their positions were reversed.

And, on top of this, another thought made him catch his breath. The old man looked up. 'I was remembering ...' he said. 'Les Treize Jours: the priest saying, "In the beginning was the Word, and the Word was with God ..."'

The other gestured. 'The Gospel according to St. John. But at Bellac "the Word" means the old knowledge, the old pagan religion.'

'And on the grave in the forest: your father's grave.'

' "The Twelve dance on high," you mean? It is from the Apocrypha, the outcast of the Bible. Why outcast? In this case because it is Jesus Christ who is dancing, and because the Apostles were not the only dancers to be twelve in number; the inmost circle of the oldest religion—call them witches if you like—was made up of twelve: of twelve and the god round whom they danced. That was a little too obvious for the Church to Christianize. They simply excommunicated it.'

'Les Treize Joueurs: the twelve dancers, and the god.'

'Exactly. But you must understand that to men like Père Dominique and Luchard and my son, Bellac's festival of the Thirteen is ... how shall I put it? Is debased. The people have always leaned towards the old witch cult. What you saw yesterday in the village is no longer pure, yet it goes hand in hand with the deeper secrets. And ...' The old voice faltered. 'And ... at certain times, it is the people who demand ...'

He seemed confused or afraid suddenly. Lindsay watched him control himself. It seemed to take a great effort of the will.

'It is their god who demands ...' He shook his head. 'The dancing god,' he concluded. And again he crossed himself.

Lindsay thought, Ah yes, the dancing god. And at the memory of the song, of the golden mask half-animal, half-human, he could not repress a shudder.

Then, suddenly, blazing through his muddled thoughts like a flame through dry grass, he saw where all this led. He jumped to his feet.

The old eyes were brilliant, looking up at him. 'Yes,' he said. 'They crucified Jesus Christ. And at Bellac that too has another meaning; in all the old religions the god was killed ...'

'To renew the earth,' said Lindsay staring out towards the distant sea, but seeing only the ruined vineyards of Bellac.

'More than one of your kings in England died in this way.'

'Rufus.'

'Yes. Among others.'

Lindsay turned, his eyes wild. 'Killed by an arrow while out hunting. I must stop them.'

'Don't be a child. Philippe has elected to die.'

'He can escape. You did; so can he.'

The old man shook his head. 'Too late. The first of August is merely the first of August to you; at Bellac it is Lammas.'

Lindsay moved towards the French windows, but a hot, dry hand gripped his wrist. 'Don't you see, boy; they won't let you stop him now. He has given them the sign that he is willing ...'

It was as if door upon door were opening in Lindsay's mind. He cried out, 'When he kissed the child! The Kiss of Peace!'

'Yes.'

'He was passing on his . . . his leadership, his power.'

The old man nodded.

'As your father did to you.'

'As my father *tried* to do to me.'

Lindsay snatched his arm away from those restraining fingers and wrenched at the handle of the French window. 'I *will* stop it,' he cried, and he was already blundering across the darkened room.

He heard the man behind him shouting, 'No. They'll know who told you. Come back. Mohammed! Mohammed, where are you?'

But the Arab must have been dozing. Lindsay caught a glimpse of him, blinking and barefooted, as he slammed out of the heavy wooden door and into the street. He heard the nurse exclaiming in her petrified genteel accent, 'Well, I *must* say . . .'

It was not until he reached Marseilles that he remembered the piece of paper in his pocket on which Françoise had written the number of her personal telephone at Bellac.

It was now four o'clock, and he fancied that already the sky was growing a little paler, though it might, he knew, be merely the lights of the city and the port catching the undersides of the thick clouds that were billowing in from the west.

Lammas, he thought, driving along the wide, brilliantly lit, totally deserted streets. Lammas. How absurd it sounded here and now! He spoke it aloud to the giant concrete blocks of offices, to the massive tiers of apartment houses where thousand upon thousand of ordinary, hard-working city-dwellers were sleeping one above the other like so many cards in so many giant filing cabinets. And yet, he thought again, who could tell what lurked in the minds of those thousand upon thousand of ordinary, hard-working city-dwellers—

what shadows of a past of which they were no longer aware? In those apartment houses lay sleeping how many men and women who had killed, or would kill, how many who housed in their bodies those legacies of the past which have been labeled perversions? Was Lammas, was Bellac, really so extraordinary? And who, looking around him on this first day of a bright new August, would not agree with those early Christian heretics that if God was good then how could he have created a world so notably evil?

Lammas. There were moments when he had to shake his head violently to make sure that he was not still lying in his bed at Bellac—that the whole of what he had heard on this night, the whole of what he had apparently lived, was not a continuing dream, heavily influenced by Mother Blossac's poppy brew. It was not true—it *could* not be true—that Philippe de Montfaucon, a more than ordinarily civilized man, intended to die on the cloudy August day that was soon to dawn. And yet thousands of men *had* died for their religion. It was no longer very fashionable, but it was certainly less stupid than dying for what was euphemistically called 'one's country,' which usually meant an egotistical and probably bone-headed group of third-rate politicians.

But, no. *No!* Philippe de Montfaucon was not going to die because he, James Lindsay, was going to see that he didn't. And yes, it *was* impossible; the whole thing was as impossible as some esoteric undergraduate spoof—half deadly serious, half bitter joke.

Was it? Had those men in the forest been joking when they had hunted him for his life? The shadow of an old man sitting on the windy terrace under the swinging light had said, 'But don't you see, boy, they won't let you stop him now?' They! 'Oh, they, they!' Françoise had said. 'Who are they?'

Lindsay, seeing in his mind's eye the tough brown people of the valley, knew that these were *they*. These had suffered from three years of famine; their crops had withered, their vines had rotted, their faith had made them turn, as they had turned for centuries, uninterrupted by the teaching of Christ's church, towards the god who would die for them, as he had always died for them.

Sweating with fear as he drove, Lindsay began to comprehend the ineluctable, deeply atavistic force—where the tonsured priest and the witch walked hand in hand—that was driving Philippe de Montfaucon to an accepted death.

He must, he *must* warn Françoise.

He stopped at a garage and, while the car was being refueled, went into a telephone booth. He suspected that Françoise would not be sleeping very soundly, if at all, on this eve of Lammas.

There was a certain lethargy of operators at the dead hour of four in the morning, but presently he heard the ringing tone, and almost immediately her voice answered. Hearing it so close to him, a little breathless, he forgot what he wanted to say—or rather what he intended to say; what he *wanted* to say was, 'I love you.' It was as well, in view of what happened a moment later, that he resisted this urge.

He said, 'Françoise. Are you all right?'

He realized a moment too late that he had not been able to keep biting anxiety out of his voice. She said, 'Yes. Yes, I'm fine. James, what's the matter? What did he say?'

'I'll tell you later. The thing is . . . Françoise, how about the children? Gilles?'

'They're sleeping upstairs with Estelle. Maybe it was silly of me . . .'

'No. I don't think it was.'

There was a slight pause. Then, her voice a little unsteady, she said, 'Oh James, hurry back, will you? I'm frightened.'

'It's all right. I'm on my way now. Listen, my dear . . . This is going to sound dreadful over the phone, but you've got to know.'

'Know?'

'I'll be with you in about four hours, maybe a bit more. We can stop it, I'm sure we can stop it, but this is the day . . . the day that Philippe . . .'

The click on the line was distinct, maddening. He cried out, 'Hello, hello. Oh damn. *Operator!*'

A faintly nettled female voice said, 'You have been cut off, monsieur.'

'Mademoiselle, I know that.'

What he did not know was that he was never going to be reconnected because someone at Bellac had dealt with the matter, using a pair of wire cutters. It took ten minutes, ten valuable minutes, for him to become sure in his own mind that this was what had happened.

He burst out of the telephone box, wild-eyed, his forehead dewed with sweat. The garage attendant gazed at him in astonishment; gazed, also in astonishment, at the enormous tip which Lindsay, unconscious to any world now but the world of Bellac, thrust upon him; gazed, gaping, at the car's eccentric departure.

It was as if the impersonal click on the telephone had been the click of a lock opening yet another of those doors in his mind—and this one the last. Suddenly all evasions, all reasonable doubts fell away from him. Marseilles, with its wide streets and its office blocks, became the world of unreality; the first workers trudging off to the dockyards and the first buses hissing on the wet roads were phantoms of a dream, and Bellac, where a god would die, became the world of hard fact. It was his own idiocy which galled him, because he had known —as soon as he set eyes on the boy, Christian, on Cottanero, on Luchard, on the priest—that they were creatures apart from his understanding. He had known, and he had done nothing. And now Philippe would die.

As he drove, very much too fast, taking risks which he would never normally have taken, he was aware of fact after fact falling into place in his brain. He was riding with Philippe down from the vineyards, the man on horseback coming towards them. Philippe was saying to the man, 'The point is must we replant? Is this something in the vines themselves?' And what had the man replied? 'Only you will know that answer, Monsieur le Marquis.'

There had been another incident too—something which had occurred after that ride, something to do with a groom. He could not remember what it was; and in any case his memory had seized onto the books which he had found in the library. He was appalled by his own short-sightedness, the stultifying ignorance which had failed to comprehend what they had so clearly told him. 'In the past ten centuries,' he had said to Françoise, 'there's a record here of thirty-five male Montfaucons, and *fourteen of them* came to grief in what I can only call suspicious circumstances.'

How many of those fourteen, he wondered now, had died at Lammas—or on another of the old festival days? (What were they?) All Hallows, Roodmass, Candlemass. Heavens above, he himself had been struck by the fact that, whereas the Montfaucons who had died in bed or in battles were given scrupulous dates, those who had died so mysteriously were not. Surely that discovery alone should have told him half that he had needed to know? Of *course* a tree had not fallen on Gils, 1422—the tree, the sacred oak, had been a symbol; doubtless he had died, like King William Rufus of England, in front of the oak—so had Grandfather Edouard. And the bas-relief of Gils in the church ... !

Lindsay banged the steering wheel with his fist. In the carving, Gils was portrayed standing under the oak holding a cup; and the cup was the only part of the carving that was worn away: it had reminded him of the Saint's toe in St. Peter's in Rome. And why was it worn away? Because it was the cup of the Grail; and the Grail, the old man had said, 'before it became Christian, held the ancient secret of Mithra.' That was why the people of Bellac had venerated it throughout the centuries; and if those candles burning in the north transept of the old church were really there in honor of the Virgin Mary, then he, James Lindsay, was a Dutchman—for the North had been sacred for thousands of years before the East.

Fact after fact, incident after incident, slid into place in his mind as the miles slid into the speedometer.

A gray, lowering dawn had given way to somber morning by the time he reached Arles. Every minute the roads were growing busier, and his progress slower. Again and again in his mind he heard that click which had severed him so utterly, so finally from Françoise. He did not think that she would be in any actual, physical danger—not, that is to say, so long as she kept her head; and she would keep her head so long as her small boy was no further involved in whatever might, at this very minute, be happening at Bellac. Yet however savagely and however often he might repeat to himself that she was in no danger, he could not banish from his memory the soft, threatening voice singing in the wood, and the snap of the Alsatian's teeth missing his throat by inches. Just at this moment there were men at Bellac who did not need very much excuse to kill; three years of disaster had made them like this, and two thousand years of tradition.

He could understand now that what gripped the people of the valley was as immediate and as real as any other form of blood lust. It was the mood of the crowd before a bullfight; it was as savagely irresistible as an outbreak of racial hatred. Intelligent men, caught up in these cataclysms of the soul, might repudiate them afterwards; at the time they were ineluctable.

But at Bellac the madness had deeper, more dangerous roots, for it was involved with a religion—a religion so old, so fundamental, so much a part of the heritage of mankind that Christianity seemed modern by comparison.

It was this, this madness of the soul, that had caught and bound him as he had stood in the little square in front of the church watching the twelve dancers and the golden man round whom they danced. The tense expectancy of that crowd of peasants had communicated itself to his inmost being; perhaps that was why, now, he *knew*, without a shadow of doubt, that the only cure for the madness was the same as it had been since the beginning of man—the spilling of blood.

With this clarity in his mind came a sense of reality. He was quite sure suddenly of what he had to do. Alone he would be helpless in the face of what waited for him at Bellac. The proper antidote, he felt sure, was the most mundane one—the appearance, in force, of the police.

After Nimes the road began to climb; there was a mountain feeling in the air, even though the mountains themselves were hidden in lowering clouds the color of ripe figs.

Lindsay lost all count of time and distance. He only knew that, however fast he drove, however many idiotic risks he took on the twisting corners that multiplied ahead of him, he could not reach the chateau soon enough. His whole being became fixed in a point of concentration, and that point was the neat sign in the street behind the Grand Place in Dennat which read, *Gendarmerie*.

He reached the little town just after nine o'clock. In the square, under the plane trees, the market was in full swing. He had to waste precious minutes while an ancient cart laden with produce was pulled out of the gutter where one wheel had got stuck in a drain.

He jerked the car to a standstill outside the police station and leapt out. By now he had reached that point of exhaustion where the system seems to revitalize itself out of itself like some kind of nuclear reactor. It was twenty-seven hours since he had slept (if that drugged coma could be called sleep) and almost as long since he had eaten anything more substantial than a sandwich. He felt utterly uncoordinated in both speech and movement, and the wound on his forehead was throbbing crazily; and yet he was not, in any accepted meaning of the word, tired. Out of his mind, perhaps, but not tired.

Certainly he must have *looked* extraordinary, if the stare given him by the gendarme on duty at the door was anything to go by.

He lurched into the stuffy office where a sergeant was sitting behind a desk, banged his fist down on it and said, 'Listen—I need your help badly. At once.'

Since policemen all over the world seem to be like highly strung spinsters waiting to be insulted by every man they meet, the sergeant gave this dirty, wild-eyed, unshaven apparition what could be called a distinctly old-fashioned look.

'Now,' he said. 'Let us begin at the beginning. What is your name, monsieur?'

'Oh for God's sake! James Lindsay. That's got nothing to do with ...'

'On the contrary, monsieur, it has everything to do with it.' His eyes flicked away from Lindsay's face and focused on something beyond him.

Lindsay, a sudden awareness of danger tingling all over him, swung round—and found himself looking straight into the brown, amorphous eyes of Prince Rinaldo Cottanero. The smooth voice said, 'Thank you, officer. You have been most kind.'

He moved forward and gripped Lindsay's arm with fingers that surprisingly belied his physical softness.

'Philippe wants to talk to you. Please come at once.'

'*No*,' said Lindsay savagely, struggling. He turned back to the policeman. 'You've got to help me. There's going to be an accident—a fatal accident ...'

The sergeant said, 'Monsieur, you should drink less or you may find yourself in serious trouble. At least be glad that you have good friends.'

To his fury Lindsay caught the two men exchanging an understanding and pitying look.

'But ...' he began.

'And you can count yourself lucky that Monsieur le Marquis is willing to overlook the theft.'

'*Theft!*'

While Lindsay's brain was still reeling, Cottanero pulled him towards the door. A man whom he dimly recognized appeared from the passage outside and took his other arm.

He turned, shouting, 'You don't understand. This is all a trick. I ...'

Cottanero said, 'Use your intelligence. Don't you see that no one believes anything you say?'

He found himself hurried out of a side door and thrust into a large, black limousine which was waiting there, engine running. A second later he was sitting in the back seat between two sturdy, brown-faced men, and the car was moving. Cottanero had got into the front next to the driver. He now turned and slid open the glass window which separated them.

Lindsay shouted, 'You're crazy, the whole lot of you.'

'The crazy man,' replied Cottanero evenly, 'is the one whom the majority of men *think* to be crazy. That's you.'

'By God,' said Lindsay, 'you can't stop me talking forever. I'll let the whole world know what happened here.'

Cottanero sighed. 'Have you finished shouting? If you have, listen to me. I chose to sit in front because I don't intend to hold any idiotic discussions with you. You can no more prevent what is happening at Bellac than you can prevent tomorrow being the second of August. As for the future, you may say whatever you like—nobody will believe you. You are a very small man, Mr. Lindsay, and you face something that not a thousand ... not a million like you can change or destroy, or even so much as dent. This has been proved for as many centuries as mankind has been on earth.'

He closed the glass window and turned away.

The man on Lindsay's left said to the man on his right, 'It would have saved a lot of trouble if we'd killed him that evening on La Bosse.'

Lindsay glanced at the two, weather-worn faces—self-contained, peasant faces with something mysterious and secret about them. His tired brain could not for a moment be sure whether they were outsiders in his world or he in theirs; suddenly the barrier between reality and unreality, perilously insecure at the best of times, seemed to have vanished altogether.

The big car swooped down the last steep incline of that winding road along the gorge, and rounded the last corner. Immediately ahead of them, blocking the way completely was a hay wain.

It took Lindsay a few seconds to realize that this was no accident. Whether it was placed there purely to stop him, if he had decided to drive straight to the chateau, or as a measure of security against the whole outside world, he was never to know. As soon as the men in charge of it saw the limousine they ran to their horses, dragging the huge cart clear. Lindsay glimpsed impassive faces as they passed, dark eyes staring, revealing nothing.

The car plunged into the dark pine wood, and a moment later Bellac swung into view—a dark, lowering fortress against dark hills under a sky of storm. On this somber day there was not a vestige of warmth in the yellowish-gray stone, and the lake, which had been a shimmering miracle the day before, glinted with the cruel lights of burnished steel. In spite of himself Lindsay's heart sank.

And now, as the road straightened out, passing between fields and vineyards, he became aware of the people of Bellac: at first a small group of them, standing together by the roadside, turning sunburned country faces to watch the car as it passed. A little further on two men stood by a gate; then six or more outside a small house.

Suddenly Lindsay realized what was strange about them; they were all looking in the same direction—towards the castle —and in the pose of each body was an unmistakable, a terrible expectancy.

He leaned forward, staring, aware of the two men watching him without sympathy. Just before they came to the village he saw an old woman in one of the vineyards; she was kneeling among the diseased vines, bent double, her face in her hands. He was seized suddenly by a terrible urgency; it rose up in him like vomit until every nerve in his body was tingling. Sweat trickled cold in the small of his back.

He was out of the car almost before it had pulled to a stand-still in the tree-lined Cour d'Honneur.

He ran, stumbling a little, up the wide steps and in at the huge doorway.

The great hall, on this thunderous day, was dark and shadowy. It was a moment before he became aware of the group of men who stood at the far end of it, their bodies lost in the gloom, only their faces, turned to look at him, palely shining, other-worldly. He recognized the abbé's German secretary, the horseman who had stopped on the road to speak to Philippe about the vines, one or two others he had seen on the morning of Les Treize Jours or at work about the estate. None of them moved or said a word.

Lindsay turned, hearing Cottanero enter the room behind him. 'Françoise . . .' he began.

'She is perfectly all right.' From the prince's voice he sensed that he had been primed on this subject; the idea infuriated him. He said, 'I must see her—now.'

Cottanero shook his head. 'Later,' he said. 'Follow me.'

He moved towards the great staircase. Lindsay stayed where he was. Cottanero turned and looked at him with something almost like compassion. 'Mr. Lindsay, you know that I shall have you *carried* after me if you don't do as I ask.'

As he moved, something else caught his attention—something which, because of his impatience or because of the gloom, he had failed to notice before. All the men who faced him were dressed for shooting; they all carried sporting guns.

Cottanero paused at the foot of the staircase. 'It's a tradition,' he said. 'I thought you knew that. The hunt on the day after Les Treize Jours.'

'Yes,' said Lindsay bitterly. 'I knew.'

He understood now that the men standing before him in the sepia shadows of the great hall were the Twelve—or would be the Twelve when they were joined by the Abbé Luchard and Christian, the only ones who were missing.

Before the cold, almost pitying stare of those ten pairs of eyes, he felt his resolution weakening again, and he knew, with a terrible sense of his own inadequacy, that this was because he had no faith to set against the passionate faith that ruled them.

He turned and followed Cottanero up the stairs. He felt feeble, helpless. In panic he realized that he had no idea what words he could try to use when at last he stood in front of his old friend.

Cottanero led him across the wide landing at the top of the stairs, up another flight, and into the corridor which ended in the massive door of the tower. It was the Abbé Luchard who opened it. Lindsay moved forward into the spacious circular room. He heard the door being locked behind him.

Philippe de Montfaucon sat in an armchair near the window. In the passionless light of that gray day Lindsay saw at once that the refining process was still at work on the handsome, bony features; yet, where there had been torment when last he saw it, there was now peace. It was this look of peace which, finally, made his hopes shrivel and die inside him.

Père Dominique stood beside the chair, one hand resting on the back of it.

On the other side of the room, leaning on the mantelpiece, but turning to look at the intruder, was Christian. Beyond him, chin in hand, gazing at the chessboard, sat the most surprising member of the company: Odile de Caray. She glanced up at Lindsay for a moment without interest.

Philippe said, 'You made a long and, by the look of you, exhausting journey for nothing, James.'

Lindsay said, 'Françoise . . .'

'Françoise is perfectly safe. She is at the moment locked into her apartments in the same way that you, in a few minutes, will be locked in here.'

His voice was so calm, so matter-of-fact, that Lindsay felt a wild desire to grab hold of him and shake him. Instead he suddenly heard himself shouting, 'You can't do this, Philippe; it's crazy, it's meaningless . . .'

He saw the fire blaze into Père Dominique's eyes, but Philippe raised a hand and silenced the priest before he could speak.

'You don't for one moment believe that it's meaningless, James, I can tell that by your face.' He stood up and came nearer. 'I'm in no mood for arguments, I daresay you can understand that; let me just say one thing. I don't know what you were told in Hyères; I assure you that your informant knows very little; I also assure you that in a few hours' time he will no longer be a resident of the Villa Oriflamme—he will be moving to another country, and he will be using another name. I have arranged that, but even if I hadn't, his own fear would have compelled him to run away . . . again.

'It was stupid of you to go to the police; I should have thought that even you, knowing the very little that you do, would have realized that there is nothing here which they will begin to understand. I advise *you*, however, to get away from Bellac as soon as you can, after you are released from this room; your . . . foreknowledge of events will be the only sort of evidence they will have, and it may make life extremely awkward for you.'

The calm impersonality of that known, once loved voice, as much as the devastating logic of what it said, was for Lindsay the coup-de-grâce. He realized that Bellac had seized him again, within a few minutes of his crossing its threshold—seized him and conquered him. He could only whimper, 'But don't you see—you're dying for nothing.'

'I shall die for my faith, and for my people—is that nothing? Did the millions who died in the last war, will the millions who are going to die in the next, die for more?' He shook his head. 'When your turn comes, James, ask yourself, "Am I dying for what I passionately believe?" The answer will be "No." '

'You believe!' Lindsay cried out. 'You *believe* all this . . . primitive hocus-pocus?'

Philippe and the priest crossed themselves.

After a moment, after he had controlled himself, Philippe de Montfaucon said, very gently, 'Yes, my old friend, I believe. And it is our belief in a thing, mine or yours, which makes that thing—forever, or for a moment—divine.'

Lindsay was entirely unable to decide—would never, in all his life, be able to decide—whether what he saw in the face of the man confronting him was the twisted conviction of insanity or the radiant conviction of saintliness. Who can say, in any case, where the dividing line between them lies? It is as equivocal as the line between stupidity and selfless bravery, between love and hatred.

All he did know was that Philippe de Montfaucon had

long ago moved out of his own world of evasions and practical considerations—that it no longer mattered whether he was right or wrong. What mattered was that he had made a choice, and that he believed, with everything that was in him, in the rightness of that choice. The belief, the strength of the belief, created its own truth.

Presumably, at this last moment, as their eyes met for the last time, Philippe was satisfied with the glimmering of understanding which he saw, because he nodded to himself.

Then, swiftly, he turned away and went to the far corner of the room where, Lindsay now noticed, there was a prie-dieu; he knelt down for a moment in prayer. Then he stood up and turned to the door; he went out without so much as a glance at Lindsay. The Abbé Luchard followed him.

Père Dominique looked at Christian, and it was now, as the boy turned from the mantelpiece, that the final pieces of the puzzle fell into place in Lindsay's mind. Something about the smooth, young face made his breath catch in his throat—an extraordinary look of ... yes, of what could only be called witless peace.

Père Dominique said to Odile de Caray, 'Is he all right?'

She nodded, turning those extraordinary amber eyes towards the young man.

Lindsay remembered that strange scene in the forecourt of the palace on the day that he had ridden with Philippe to look at the vineyards: how the groom had moved to take his master's horse, and how he had seemed almost ashamed of this natural action when Christian had intervened. He remembered, too, that little outbreak of jeering—and yet it had been only a token jeering—which the young man's presence in front of the church had called forth from the crowd. He remembered, finally, how in drawing that face he had been surprised to find evidence of the primitive characteristics underlying the surface sophistication.

He saw, quite clearly now, that the boy was under deep hypnosis, and he understood, as perhaps he had always understood with some instinctive part of his own mind—and as the people of Bellac had certainly known from the beginning—that it was this boy in this state who would kill Philippe de Montfaucon under the oak tree in the forest on the day of Lammas. The beloved would kill the god, just as William Rufus had been killed by his familiar, Tyrrell.

And so the circle was completed. Odile de Caray completed it at this moment when she, the priest, and the young man, smiling a little, walked out of the room, and out of his life.

He heard the key turn in the lock.

Now there was absolute silence over the whole castle. Lindsay thought that it was as if he had been struck deaf; he made himself walk across the room to hear the sound of his own footsteps. The movement took him to the window, so that, almost in spite of himself, he saw them ride out. There was a clatter of hooves, a jingle of stirrups, and then, beyond the gate house and the drawbridge, the cavalcade moved into view; he could see Philippe in front, and behind him the Twelve. Christian was immediately recognizable, not only for the unconscious grace with which he sat his horse, but for the fact that whereas all the others carried guns, he alone carried the sturdy longbow which had been in his hand when Lindsay had first seen him.

The horsemen moved away along the side of the lake; timeless they looked from this distance, as they trotted towards the dark forest under the leaden sky.

And then, once more, he became aware of the people of Bellac: first of all, in the courtyard below him, castle servants presumably—a group of five, staring after the riders; and there, at the edge of the formal garden, two figures straightened up from their work, heads turned towards the lake. A groom appeared in the archway leading to the stables; he spoke over his shoulder to someone behind him, and a moment later another groom joined him, wiping his hands on a piece of rag; a small boy ran out after them, looking up at them, questioning; the men glanced at each other, and then laughed at the child, shaking their heads. And perhaps it was that look and that laugh which told Lindsay, more than words could ever tell about the conspiracy of silence which ruled the valley—a conspiracy from which both he and the child were excluded; for them, for those who did not know or did not believe, what was about to happen would be 'an accident while out hunting'; for the others . . .

He saw movement in the village now: more people of Bellac were coming out of their houses, out of their barns, looking up from the neat rows of their diseased vines or from the sickly yellow patches of their corn, to watch the thirteen horsemen —the twelve and the one—who rode towards the forest.

Much later—he could not have told how long he sat there in the utterly silent room—Lindsay heard the sound of the door being unlocked. For a moment his dazed mind did not quite grasp what it meant. Then he was on his feet and running.

It was as he reached the landing at the top of the staircase that the dog began to howl. The sound, shattering that silence, brought him to a standstill, the hair crawling on the nape of his neck. The Great Dane was standing in the shadows of the hall below, head raised in lament. Lindsay knew then that somewhere in the forest the arrow had been loosed.

He turned and flung himself at the door across the landing. He had half-expected it to be locked, but it was not. The first thing he noticed was that Françoise had closed the shutters and drawn the curtains; she stood in the middle of the lamp-lit room, staring at him.

He ran to her and took her in his arms, holding her closely; he was saying, 'I couldn't stop him. Forgive me—there was nothing I could do . . .'

Almost savagely Françoise said, 'Don't tell me, James; I don't want to hear. Please, please don't tell me.' But her arms around him tightened their grip.

So they stood there, in the room with the closed shutters—a flimsy wooden barrier against a savage day which they could neither of them understand.

Below, in the hall, the howling dog was suddenly quiet.

13

The Waiting Valley

Prince Cottanero had said to Lindsay, 'You can no more prevent what is happening than you can prevent tomorrow being the second of August. As for the future, you may say whatever you like—nobody will believe you.'

During the days that followed the death of Philippe de Montfaucon Lindsay had ample opportunity to realize that the prince had been quite right. There were times when he even doubted his *own* sanity.

The official inquiry into the death was conducted with respect and tact. To Lindsay it was like a bad dream—one of those nightmares in which everything one knows to be true is subtly changed to a falsehood. The gentleman in charge of the proceedings was small, elegant, white-haired. He had clearly been warned in advance that the English witness, James Lindsay, was slightly eccentric and might, given the chance, rob the inquiry of all its dignity. He never gave the English witness, James Lindsay, any such chance.

It might be thought, he said, that someone had been distinctly lax to allow a young man like Christian, of a noticeably happy-go-lucky disposition, to go out shooting with, of all things, a bow and arrow which it was clear he was unable to control with any degree of proficiency. The terrible contrition which the young man was now suffering, and the fact that he was clearly unsure exactly how the fatal arrow had come to be loosed were two points beyond question. It seemed, he said, that the whole tragedy might more properly be called the fault of the adults who were present, rather than of the unfortunate young man himself. (A good deal of publicity was given to the fact that his father was a saintly, near-legendary figure who was giving his life to the lepers in Africa.) On the whole people felt rather sorry for Christian. Nobody felt in the least sorry for Lindsay.

This odd character, it was pointed out, was not only an Englishman but also an artist. (Everybody thought this a highly amusing conjunction.) He appeared to have spent much of his time at the chateau reading the history of the Montfaucon family. Now it was undeniable that many of the deceased's ancestors had died in odd circumstances: three of them, by a strange quirk of coincidence, on August the first, the same day as the late marquis. This may have given rise to the well-attested fact that the Englishman, Lindsay, actually spoke of the accident *before* it happened. Since the last Montfaucon death, prior to the one under inquiry, to fall on this date had been in the year 1624, it was generally thought that the Englishman's prognostication had been a very long shot indeed.

If Lindsay seemed to behave in a rather excitable way under inquiry, most charitable people put it down to the 'artistic temperament' and to the fact that two days before the accident he had fallen off his horse and severely injured his head. It was noticed that the widowed marquise watched him with a good deal of trepidation and was seen, on more than one occasion, urging him to calm down.

The inquiry was inclined to pooh-pooh most of the statements made by the ordinary people of Bellac. There were, it admitted, certain rather odd details which were not easily explained. For instance, it seemed quite unnecessary to carry the body of the deceased halfway round the estate before taking it back to the castle, but Bellac was something of a backwater, and it had to be remembered that peasants had their own ancient traditions in these matters. (Lindsay at this juncture thought that he had indeed gone quite mad. But then all such obvious pointers to the death having been a ritual killing were completely ignored.)

The evidence of the old woman, Jeanne Defranc, who had stated that the blood of the deceased dripped over every inch of the way, was discounted entirely. Medical men had stated that this was an impossibility. (Lindsay groaned aloud, and was stared at pityingly.)

The inquiry concluded its findings by saying that no one should be led astray by the marked difference in attitude shown by the people of Bellac towards the death. It might seem that some of them held the late marquis in a degree of esteem which almost bordered on adulation; but then it had to be remembered that he had been an excellent landlord.

At the end of all this, the small, white-haired gentleman in charge of proceedings fixed Lindsay with a beady brown eye, and added a rider. It was possibly just as well, he said—in view of his foreknowledge of his friend's death—that the Englishman, James Lindsay, had, at the time of the death, locked himself by accident into a remote and little-used part of the chateau. Particularly in view of the fact that James Lindsay had, most unexpectedly, been named as principal legatee in the will.

And now ... Now Françoise and James live in a very beautiful old farmhouse not far from Lorient on the coast of Brittany. As most people will know, he is now an internationally recognized painter; there is not a gallery interested in contemporary work which does not possess at least one of his paintings. He and Françoise are very happy, and the four children are delightful.

Tante Estelle often visits them. (Her brother, Philippe's father, died two years ago.) She divides her time between the farmhouse in Brittany and her own small apartment in Paris.

James is still not sure in his own mind whether or not he should have taken the whole matter further; whether or not he should have exposed the inquiry for the short-sighted farce which it assuredly was. Françoise and Tante Estelle are both quite sure; it was they who persuaded him to keep quiet—for the memory of a man whom they had all loved, and for the sake of Gilles and Antoinette.

Gilles is now sixteen. He knows that he is the possessor of an ancient title and the vast estates that go with it. He remembers Bellac well, but shows no inclination to go back there. He has a brilliant head for figures, and there is a plan afoot for him to enter the Swiss banking house to which, via his maternal grandmother, he is related.

Françoise and James, though surprised by this ambition, are not altogether displeased. They can think of nothing further removed from the baleful influence of Bellac than the money factories of Basel. And yet . . . And yet . . .

The chateau stands empty, lapped in its own immutable silence. The brown people of the valleys go about their business, thinking their secret thoughts. There have been many years of abundance now, and hardly a week goes by without a fresh posy of flowers, a bunch of grapes, a twist of corn being placed upon the gravestone of Philippe de Montfaucon.

Sometimes you may see one of the men pause in his weeding, one of the women glance up from her scrubbing, to look at the empty road which leads down into the valley from that other world outside.

It will not, they know, always be empty. Soon or late, next year or in ten years' time, another will come. Until that day they will wait in patience.

The Twelve dance on high, Amen.

The whole on high hath part in our dancing. Amen.

Whoso danceth not, knoweth not what cometh to pass. Amen.

CPSIA information can be obtained at www.ICGtesting.com
Printed in the USA
LVOW11s1525280316

481072LV00004B/473/P